"I care about you and your dad, and about the orchard," Toby said.

"I always have, Jenna," he continued. "You guys are a second family to me."

Jenna turned away. "Don't say stuff you don't mean."

He stood just inches from her, his gaze searching hers with an intensity she couldn't look away from.

"I care, Jenna. I care. Tell me what I have to do to prove it and I will."

Wrestling her racing heartbeat, Jenna fought the need to sag against him. To rest her head against his chest, cling to him and cry for all their lost years. But Toby didn't love her. Never would. He'd made that fact crystal clear years ago—his friendship with her was a dirty secret he didn't want anyone to know about. She wouldn't fall for that again. For him and his ability to say the right thing.

Besides, even if he was a changed man…she had changed, too.

"I want things to be okay between us again," he whispered with a gentleness that tore at her heart.

Could she ever trust him?

Jessica Keller is a Starbucks drinker, avid reader and chocolate aficionado. Jessica holds degrees in communications and biblical studies. She is multipublished in both romance and young-adult fiction and loves to interact with readers through social media. Jessica lives in the Chicagoland suburbs with her amazing husband, beautiful daughter and two annoyingly outgoing cats who happen to be named after superheroes. Find all her contact information at jessicakellerbooks.com.

Books by Jessica Keller

Love Inspired

Goose Harbor

Lone Star Cowboy League: Boys Ranch

Apple Orchard Bride

Jessica Keller

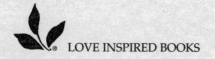 LOVE INSPIRED BOOKS

Recycling programs for this product may not exist in your area.

ISBN-13: 978-0-373-62251-1

Apple Orchard Bride

Copyright © 2016 by Jessica Koschnitzky

www.Harlequin.com

Printed in U.S.A.

For Carol, who has never given up on me.
Not once. Not ever.
Thank you for being one of my heart sisters.

The Lord is near to the brokenhearted
and saves the crushed in spirit.
—*Psalms* 34:18

Chapter One

"This can't be happening." Jenna Crest jogged toward the line of dwarf trees she'd planted at her family orchard when she'd first moved back in with her father.

Young branches were stripped bare, and chunks of bark had been peeled off at least eleven of her sixteen new Braeburn trees. With damp dirt between her fingers, Jenna scrambled from tree to tree, desperately trying to determine if any of them could be saved. Even though she knew the answer right away, she still examined each one closer. All were ruined.

Much like her.

She stood, rested her hands on her hips and kicked at the ground. "All that work. For what? Nothing."

These new trees had cost her countless hours of care, attention and even love. She'd researched and chosen the breed of trees, despite her father suggesting they plant Pristine trees along the edge of their property. She'd tested the soil's pH and had dug sulfur into the row until it reached the correct level.

Whole days during the hottest portion of the past summer had been devoted to training the branches to grow correctly—tying them together to help the tree maintain the best shape for bearing the most fruit in years to come. She'd pruned and encouraged the branches and made special trips out at dusk just to recheck them before nightfall—even though going out at night caused panic to tickle up her spine. Jenna had battled the codling moths to keep her baby trees safe and had worried for weeks as she treated other plants in the orchard for apple scab, knowing that if the tiny trees caught the common disease, they'd be wiped out.

None of it mattered. Despite her best efforts, deer had come in the night and destroyed any chance the trees had of one day bearing fruit. She'd done everything right, yet still they were damaged beyond repair.

Story of her life.

Jenna swiped at the burning tears waiting to fall. Tears wouldn't bring back the dying trees and couldn't help her situation. They hardly ever did. She'd cried herself dry over the years, and the practice had never healed her. For that matter, neither had God. Wasn't He supposed to care about His followers? If not her, then He should at least care about her father. Dad had been a God-fearing man his whole life. He'd raised her to know God and had loved his wife fiercely until the moment her soul slipped beyond life. Yet all of her father's devotion to God had led to his being diagnosed with a debilitating condition. It didn't make sense.

Honestly, not much did.

Fairness in this life was a fantasy.

Jenna sighed. *Move. Stop thinking. It doesn't do any good anyway.*

She might not be able to untangle the ways of God, but she could determine the cause of the damaged trees.

Stepping away from the row of Braeburns, she crossed over to the fence that enclosed the orchard. They referred to it as a deer fence because even though it looked simply like two thin lines of metal, they were charged. With the entire orchard being made up of dwarf trees that stood between only six and eight feet high, an electric fence was the only way to keep their harvest safe from being picked clean by pests. The deer must have found a weak spot.

Crouching toward the nearest patch of fence, Jenna angled her head, trying to listen for the telltale hum of electricity. Nothing. She reached to touch the line.

"You know better than to touch that." A familiar, honey-smooth voice caused her muscles to jolt. Jenna lost her crouched position, her knees dropping into the longer grass.

Toby. It was Toby Holcomb's voice.

That couldn't be right though. Toby lived clear across the country, all the way in Florida. One of the best things about coming back to Goose Harbor this time around was knowing she'd never run into him again. Not after his parents moved out of town. He had zero reason to ever return to Michigan.

Still, her pulse picked up as a thousand shared childhood memories collided in her mind. The kid from across the street. The boy she'd built a tree house with. They used to run through the orchard at night, playing flashlight tag. A best friend who… But it couldn't be him. He'd left town—left her—at eighteen and never looked back.

Jenna craned her neck and spotted him, less than fifteen feet away, closing the distance quickly. That was Toby, all right. Her heart pounded up into her throat.

She swallowed hard and rubbed her palms against the thighs of her jeans. He couldn't be here. She didn't want him nearby.

That didn't fit with her plan.

She squinted against the glare of the rising autumn sun. Even as a teenager, Toby had been handsome, an all-American boy with a heaping dose of superhero good looks thrown in for good measure. His hair was the same as before, a mix of brown and blond, the kind of color women paid a lot of money in salons to achieve. From the way his T-shirt pulled across his frame, the past ten years had given him tighter arm muscles and firmer shoulders. Despite the upper bulk on his frame, the rest of him—strong legs, athletic stride—was built for speed. A reminder that he'd played running back for a Division I school. He'd been a shoo-in to be drafted onto a professional football team until his career-ending injury during his final season in college. His eyes were a refreshing, crisp blue, like a cloudless fall day in the height of harvest time.

For the space of a heartbeat, as memories and lost hopes crashed around in her mind, words left her.

The first man to ever betray her. She should have learned her lesson. He should have been the first and last to hurt her. If only. She couldn't change the past, but going forward, Toby wouldn't get another opportunity to cause her pain. Never again.

Recovering from the shock of seeing him, she gulped in a fortifying breath and then leaned forward, toward the fence. "You, of all people, don't get to tell me what I can and can't do." She tapped the wire with her pointer finger, and a shudder of power surged through her arm. That part of the fencing was very much alive.

Toby stopped less than three feet away from her. He smirked, crossed his arms and shook his head in a mocking way. "See? I'm guessing that hurt."

The fuzzy feeling of electricity hummed around her elbow. "I'm fine." She'd brushed the fence countless times in her life; the charge was far too weak to actually cause pain, and the feeling would be gone in a few minutes. She started to rise. Toby grabbed her arm to help her up, but she shrugged away from his touch. Dealing with him close-up hurt far more than any electrical zap could.

A part of her wanted to shove his chest and yell at him. *You ruined my life! You were the catalyst that started it all!* But telling him that would only give him power because it would reveal how much he'd once meant to her. She'd been in love with a fool. A fool who had never given her a second thought.

Jenna took a step back, creating more distance between them. "Why are you here?"

His lips tugged to an almost smile, but his lowered brows betrayed his confusion. "It's good to see you, too."

She copied his cross-armed stance. "Answer the question."

He dropped his arms to his sides, tilting his palms up to reveal the smallest of shrugs. "It was time to come home."

Home? As in…he was staying in Goose Harbor for good? No. Jenna didn't want to—couldn't—deal with running into him all the time. Not when he reminded her of past hopes, the time before the bad, and also why everything went wrong in her life to begin with. How could she heal when the man who inflicted the first puncture wound to her soul was nearby?

"Your parents don't live here anymore." *So why are you here?* The Holcombs had sold their home five years ago. Toby had no reason to be in Goose Harbor.

He nodded. "They love that retirement community. Florida suits them well."

Jenna pressed her fists into her armpits. "But not you?"

Toby scrubbed his palm against his jawline. "Even after almost ten years in the Sunshine State, it's not my place. Goose Harbor's the only place that wins the *home* label."

Her mouth went dry, but she forced out the words anyway. "Well, I can't speak for the rest of town, but you're certainly not welcome on our property."

Toby cocked his head. "He didn't tell you?"

Her gaze finally connected with his. Which was a mistake. A huge one. She'd avoided looking him in the eye until now, but she'd have a hard time looking away. "You know I hate when you ask leading questions. Spit it out."

"Your dad hired me. I work here now." He hooked his thumb over his shoulder in the direction of the farm-house. "In fact, I'm living in the bunkhouse."

"Since—" her voice faltered "—since when?"

"Moved in last night." He studied her. Almost as if he was waiting for her to smile or be friendly. Then he sighed. "The lights were off at your place so I figured you guys were out."

It felt like the air had been sucked from her lungs. An ache rocked through her chest. *Do not have a panic attack. Not now. Not here. Not in front of him.*

"No," she whispered.

"Jenna." Toby's voice was soft and warm as he took a step closer. "Your dad needs help."

"I'm here." She narrowed her gaze and pressed her hand into her chest. "I help him."

"And run this place, too?" He tossed out his hands, encompassing the whole orchard. "All by yourself? Why? I spent every summer during junior high and high school working for him, taking care of this place."

"Yeah, and then you left on the back of a convertible, waving like a hero from the town parade, and never looked back." She spun on her heels, determined to flee from the situation before an attack brought her to her knees. She needed to be alone and mentally review what had just happened. Figure out a plan for coping with seeing Toby again.

But Toby caught her arm. "You're angry." He said it like it was some huge revelation. As if he hadn't been the one to pretend to be her friend when it was just the two of them but then made fun of her in public, causing the final two years of high school to be some of the most miserable of her life.

She shoved his hand off her arm and squared her shoulders. "I'd have to actually care to be angry, but when it comes to you and your life, hear this—I don't care."

Toby watched Jenna stalk through the grass away from him. A penny toad and a couple grasshoppers fled from her steps.

Oh. She was mad. She was so mad she couldn't stand to look at him.

That was unexpected.

"Jen-na," he groaned, dragging out the two syllables in her name, just like the old days.

She picked up her speed.

Despite the fact, or possibly because of the fact, that Jenna had been homeschooled for most of her childhood, she'd been Toby's best friend. Toby's entire childhood was a wash of his parents caring for his brother, trying to help Ben fight the leukemia that had eventually taken his life. It could have been lonely, but the Crest family—Jenna in particular—had made sure his days were full of laughter and friendship. She'd always been a beacon of hope in his life, just waiting across the street. Because she was homeschooled, he'd been able to make their friendship this safe and secret thing that was only for him. None of his friends at the public school knew about Jenna, and he'd liked it that way. She was his. Special. The one person he didn't have to pretend with.

When her mother died during their junior year of high school, Jenna's dad had to enroll her in the public high school. The school Toby attended. His school friends had consisted of other guys on the football team and the girls who trailed after that type. Jenna was always shy to the point of being silent in large groups and had worn outfits made out of pleated resale-shop jeans and flowery tops that were appropriate for grade school children. She'd had a braid that hung well past her lower back. A rumor had worked its way through school during her first week there that she was half-Amish. She had worn thick purple-rimmed glasses and had a mouth full of braces back then. His group would have ridiculed her every single day if they had known he and she were best friends.

They would have ridiculed him, too.

But he'd *protected* her by not letting his school friends know they were close. He'd saved her from so much grief and teasing that public knowledge of their friendship would have brought on her. At least, his actions had made sense back in high school. She knew that, right? Ten years had passed since graduation.

No one was stubborn enough to hang on to hurt for that long.

Then again, Jenna had once not spoken for two weeks when they were ten or eleven years old because he'd dared her that she wouldn't be able to. Perhaps people could do anything they put their minds to, even if their minds were set on holding on to something toxic.

"Wait up!" He started after her at a jog. Leaves rustled, and a branch scraped against his arm as he cut through a row of trees in order to catch up.

She kept her eyes fixed on the barn and farmhouse in the distance. "Leave me alone, Toby."

"I can't. Not when I'm going to be living a stone's throw from your house for the foreseeable future." He tried to infuse his smile with a measure of warmth, hoping to thaw her mood. "That's even closer than when we were across-the-street neighbors. Neither of us ever imagined that would happen one day, did we?"

"Stop chatting about the old days as if we're still friends."

"Aren't we?" His voice squeaked. Why did his voice squeak?

Sure, he hadn't called or written in ten years—but then, neither had she. His parents talked to her dad regularly, so she could have gotten Toby's information if she had wanted it. Evidently, she hadn't. Women were like that though, weren't they? For them to consider someone a friend, it seemed as if they had to talk weekly and catch up. Come to think of it, Toby's mom always bugged him about returning her calls. Men could not talk for twenty years, bump into an old buddy fishing and suddenly act like they hadn't missed any time. Men didn't need all the "Why didn't you ever call?" nonsense.

Jenna stopped in her tracks and glared at him. "Listen, you might as well go pack your things because I'm going to talk to my father, and when I'm done, he's going to un-offer you that position."

Her hands were fisted at her sides. She looked like she might start yelling. Which wasn't like the Jenna from his memories. She'd always been smiling, quick to tease him but also the first and most constant encourager in his life. For a long time, she'd been the only one who believed he was good enough to become a professional athlete.

Unfortunately, he'd ended up disappointing everyone. Especially Jenna.

Maybe returning to Goose Harbor had been a mistake. Even still, they both knew Mr. Crest would never toss him out after offering him a job and a place to stay. Jenna's dad was a man of his word.

"You know that—"

"We don't need more help on the orchard." She lifted her chin. "I'm doing just fine on my own, and we always hire seasonal help once harvest gets into full swing anyway."

Toby's gaze raked over her. Frustration had always made her appealing, but there was something more that captured his attention today. Her pale cheeks became the color of sunset pink. Her dark blue eyes deepened, like the crashing waves of Lake Michigan right before a storm. Gone was his awkward once-best friend. She was replaced by a gorgeous woman with thick eyelashes and wavy golden curls. The pleated jeans were now dark-wash ones that accentuated the curve of her hips and the narrowing of her waist, and the Crest Orchard T-shirt she wore hugged her torso. Jenna had grown up to become a beautiful woman.

She leaned her head forward and arched her eyebrow. "You have nothing to say? Absolutely nothing?"

Right. He should have said something, but his mouth had gone dry. What was she asking if he had anything to say about? Was she referring to her threat to get her father to fire him, or was she trying to get him to talk about something…deeper? Knowing Jenna, it was the second.

He swallowed hard. "I'm sorry. For whatever it is I did to upset you, I'm sorry."

"For whatever it is I did." She mimicked his voice. "Nice, Toby. Real nice. I should have known you'd never own up to anything."

"I'd be happy to own up to it if I knew what you were talking about."

"So what happened? Huh?" She cocked her head to the side. "You finally messed up your life so badly down there in Florida that you had to come crawling back here to our *podunk farm* and beg for a job. Life is funny, isn't it?" She lifted her hands, palms up, to indicate him. "Here you are…stuck in a place you openly scorned."

Confusion tied his gut in a knot. "Jenna…"

"I suppose even a place and people you consider beneath you is better than jail though, right?"

Excellent. So she knew about his drunk-driving arrests, too. He had a huge hill to climb in order to convince people in Goose Harbor that he wasn't *that* Toby anymore. "They don't actually keep you in jail. You get out on bond," he mumbled.

"You don't remember, do you?" She laughed once, but the sound held no humor. "I guess something like spreading rumors about the poor, backward folk who lived across the street from you is an understandable slip of the mind. The great Toby Holcomb leaves a big wake and never looks back."

At least she wasn't focusing on his arrests. But...what *was* she talking about? "I've never said—"

"Don't try to deny it. I heard you. More than once, I overheard you telling people about the orchard." Jenna worked her tiny jaw back and forth. She cupped her hand over her forehead and released a long sigh. "None of that matters now. That was a long time ago. You've moved on. I've moved on. So...let's keep with that notion and move you out of here." She turned away and started for the farmhouse again.

Toby kept pace with her but didn't say anything. What could he say? Nothing. Sometimes silence was the best option. He'd use the next few weeks to unravel the reasons Jenna was so upset with him, and then he'd spend the weeks after that making up for his wrongs, no matter if they were real or only perceived.

He couldn't accept the fact that she might not forgive him or that things couldn't go back to how they were before. They had to. He wanted to make her laugh again and suddenly longed to find their old haunts and set out on new adventures together. Dream about their futures, as they'd done before. Here at the orchard, they were somehow sheltered from the real world and the issues in their lives from the past years. He was able to breathe deeply here, and he felt more like himself than he'd felt...since he left. And Jenna was a part of that, wasn't she? Even with ten years of distance between them, she knew him better than anyone else alive.

He'd make things right between them. He had to. Because as he walked beside her through the orchard again—even with the two of them at odds—his heart had never felt more at home. Perhaps that's why his relationships in Florida had never worked, had never felt right.

His heart had been stuck in Goose Harbor all along.

Chapter Two

Jenna felt like she was going to throw up.

Why wouldn't Toby go away? *Just. Go. Away.*

A charge buzzed over her skin as if she were still touching the electric fence. He was invading *her* safe place. Her escape. Her mind instantly flew to a darker place. To a date in college with a very different man, who had invaded not only her space but her body, taking her innocence and destroying her faith in other people in one night.

She'd survived the past eight years since then by carefully constructing a life that kept her safe and protected at all times. Only interacting with other people on her terms—like at church or the farmers' market or at the Bible study she attended—and then spending the rest of her time locked away. Alone. Safe.

The only man she really trusted was her father. He was the only one she was okay with being near. Toby living on her dad's property messed up her protected space. She couldn't feel secure here if she had to worry about running into him all the time. Not that Toby would harm her physically—she didn't believe that of her old friend for one second—but the feeling of invasion made her gasp for air all the same.

A line of sweat slipped down her spine. They were in for another hot day.

Her father didn't know, would never know, about the assaults that happened to her during college. He wouldn't be able to comprehend why Jenna was so vehemently opposed to Toby living in the bunkhouse. The only way to get Dad to agree would be to tell him about the horrible things she'd overheard Toby say about his beloved orchard all those years ago and hope it fired Dad up enough to tell Toby to take a hike. Although... Dad could be frustratingly full of grace and forgiveness. It was a trait she had admired and loved about him until this very moment.

When she rounded the edge of the last row of trees, her two-story white farmhouse came into view. Although, instead of the normal, peaceful feelings that the sight of her family home usually brought, she zeroed in on all that was wrong with it. The house hadn't been painted in years, probably because Dad had been declining for longer than anyone—even he—realized. Huge chunks of white were missing from sections of the lower portion of the house, and both sets of stairs and the front and side overhangs drooped. The gray-green roof had seen better days. The state of the house resembled Toby's high school statements about the Crests being podunk and backward.

"I want to stay." Toby's voice broke through her thoughts. "I want to help here."

"We don't need you." She sped up her stride, making it to the back steps a moment later. She yanked open the screen door, and it shuttered on its ancient frame. "Dad!" she called. "We need to talk."

A bowl of oatmeal sat untouched and cold at the kitchen table. She glanced at the digital numbers on the oven. Almost nine in the morning. She'd been out longer than she'd planned, but Dad should have finished eating by now.

Worry gnawing at the back of her mind, Jenna left the kitchen and made for the front of the house. Because it was built more than a hundred years ago, there was no such thing as an open floor plan in their farmhouse, just little divided areas.

"Dad!" Her voice grew louder. Why wasn't he answering?

Jenna all but ran into the front sitting room and screamed when she saw her father lying, facedown, on the floor. Chunks of a broken mug were scattered near where one of his hands rested in a pool of coffee, but more concerning was the small puddle of red near where his forehead rested.

"Dad! No! No! No!" she yelled and fell to her knees beside him. She touched his shoulder. Still warm. Alive. *Thank You, God.*

"Toby!" she screamed. "Toby, help!" The infuriating man had followed her all over the orchard but hadn't followed her into the farmhouse. He must have heard her call, though, because his echoing steps pounded into the house.

"Jenna?" His voice lifted in question.

"Front room!" She turned her attention back to her dad. "Daddy." She tapped his shoulders again. "Please be okay. I need you to be okay." She smoothed her hand over his back. Should she move him? Flip him over? She probably wasn't strong enough to do it while still supporting his neck. That's what a person was supposed to do when someone passed out, right? Turn them on their back and start chest compressions? Or would that harm him? If something was wrong with his neck or back, movement might further injure him. She didn't want to make the decision on her own. "Toby!" she yelled again. *Hurry up!*

"Jen—" Toby's face fell when he entered the room. "What happened?" He dropped down beside her.

"I don't know. I found him like this." Her words trembled as tears started to crash down toward her chin. "I can't lose him, Tobe." Her childhood name for him slipped out before she could rein it in. She pressed on. "Will you help me roll him over?"

Toby eased closer. "Call 9-1-1. If he needs it, I know CPR."

"But—" Feeling completely out of control in the situation, she froze. She wanted to curl up in a ball and let Toby take care of everything. But Dad needed her.

"Now, Jenna. Call." Toby looked back at her father. He gently cupped where the nape of Dad's neck met his hair and flipped him onto his back. The line of blood on her dad's temple shifted to run down the side of his face. He looked as if he had on fake paint for a monster costume. On the positive side, if the gash was still bleeding, then he couldn't have been passed out long.

Toby grabbed her father's wrist and leaned close to his chest. "He has a pulse and he's breathing. Call, Jenna. Go call for help."

Dial 9-1-1. Right. Her cell phone. She felt in her pockets. She hadn't grabbed it earlier. Jenna started for the kitchen but stopped when she heard a quiet groan.

Toby smiled. "He's awake."

Her dad blinked a few times and then tried to sit up, but Toby stayed him with a hand to his shoulder. "Easy, now, Mr. Crest. You fell. We found you passed out. We're going to call an ambulance for you."

"No." Her father pressed his eyes shut and groaned again. "No ambulance. I won't leave my house that way."

Toby sent Jenna a look that said "What now?" It was only an uneven lift of his eyebrows, but she knew him well enough to know what all his facial expressions meant.

"Daddy." She slowly stepped back into the room, as if he might scare if she walked normally. "You're bleeding. You were unconscious. We need to get you to the hospital."

"Stop your worrying, the both of you." Dad started to try to rise to a sitting position again, so Toby braced his back and helped him up. Toby pulled one of the chairs closer so her father could lean against it.

Dad gingerly touched his temple. "It was nothing."

"Nothing?" Jenna arched her eyebrow. "Like your hands shaking were nothing this morning?"

"I tripped on the carpeting and knocked my head on the arm of that chair on the way down." He pointed at the curled-over edge of their large rug and the wooden armrest on one of the two antique chairs that flagged the sitting area. "That's all. It could happen to anyone. Even someone strong and fit like you or Toby."

"Even still." Toby exchanged another worried look with Jenna. "We'd like to get you to the hospital."

Her father set his jaw. "I'm not climbing into an ambulance."

"They help you into it—" Toby started to say.

Jenna shook her head. "That's not what he means." Dad could be more stubborn than dried tar. Which was probably where she got that particular trait from.

Jenna disappeared into the kitchen and grabbed her keys, her cell phone and a clean dish towel from the counter. She marched back into the sitting room and jangled the keys. "I'm driving you there." She tossed the kitchen towel to Toby. "Press that to his cut."

Toby did as instructed. And as if reading her mind, when they were ready to leave, Toby wrapped his arm around her father and helped him walk to the car.

"I'll sit in back." Dad motioned toward the backseat of her late-model Camry. "I may want to lie down."

Toby made sure her dad was buckled in. "Try not to fall back to sleep. I'm sure they'll want to check you for a concussion," he instructed before claiming the passenger seat.

Jenna started up the car and backed out of their driveway without looking over at Toby. If he hadn't been there…if she'd been all alone and something happened to her father…something worse…what would she have done? Would she have been able to clear her mind enough to call for help? She wanted the answer to that question to be yes, of course. But whenever panic clawed its way into her chest, it seemed to affect her ability to think, as well. What if something happened to her father and she couldn't help him because she was in the middle of an anxiety attack?

Toby was right. She needed another person at the orchard. She needed help.

Now to taste humble pie.

"Thank you," she whispered so only Toby could hear.

No need to stress her father out in his condition; he didn't need to know that she and Toby had been arguing.

"For?" Toby's eyebrows rose.

"Coming when I called...even after..." She swallowed hard and tried to make her voice even. "After what I said to you."

"Listen." He angled his body so he was leaning over the middle control area and lowered his voice. "From what I've gathered, there's some water under the bridge that you and I need to sort through. And we will. But no matter what—and hear me on this, Jenna—no matter what happens between us, I'll always come if you call for me. Got that? Always."

She sucked in a shaky breath and nodded. Toby wanted to deal with their issues? Was that even possible? And if they did sort through everything...then what? They weren't kids running through the apple orchard any longer—they could never go back to those carefree days. After everything that had happened in both of their lives, they could never go back to their old, easy friendship.

She could accept his help on the orchard and with her father, but she couldn't welcome him back as a friend. Not ever. Not after the way he—and every guy after him—had betrayed her.

"Mr. Crest." Toby opened his visor and used the mirror on it to keep an eye on her father. "I'm going to ask you some questions to help you stay alert, okay?"

"Do your worst." Her dad's smile was soft, but his joking manner made Jenna ease her foot off the accelerator. It wouldn't help them to get a speeding ticket on the way to the hospital.

"Favorite food?"

"Besides apple pie?"

"Sure."

"Roast-beef sandwiches."

"Who's the best football team?" Toby asked with a grin.

Dad laughed. "Packers."

"You know that makes you a state traitor, right?" Toby shook his head as his grin widened.

"Oh, please." Her father crossed his arms. "Had they offered for you out of college, you would have accepted."

"You're…you're not wrong."

Had Toby flinched? Or had Jenna only imagined it?

Toby cleared his throat. "Did Kasey give you any trouble this morning?"

"Who's Kasey?" Jenna glanced in Toby's direction at the next stoplight. His pale blue eyes almost looked like they had a white electric circle in them. She forced herself to look back at the road.

Her dad leaned toward the front of the car. "She's only the cutest little girl I've ever met. Present company excluded." He tapped Jenna's shoulder and then rested his other hand on Toby's shoulder. "She was nervous about her first day of school and starting after everyone else, so she and I prayed together before she got on the bus."

"Wait." Jenna gripped the steering wheel tighter. "Who's Kasey? She was at our house? I'm so confused."

"I helped her get on the bus so Toby could start working on the orchard."

Toby nodded and then pointed toward the entrance to the hospital parking lot. Like much of the Goose Harbor area, the small hospital was nestled in by the thick forest that lined much of the dune-covered areas of town. If there weren't huge arrows and many signs for the hospital on the street leading up to the entryway, people would miss it all the time, especially when not thinking straight in an emergency.

Jenna would have never missed the entrance though. She'd driven Dad here for one too many appointments in the past six months. She could probably sleepwalk to the hospital with no problem. Which was a good thing, because Dad and Toby's discussion had distracted her.

Did Toby have a daughter?

"Wait, is Kasey *yours*?" She parked near the doorway for the ER.

Toby unbuckled his seat belt and opened his door. "In a way, yes." He closed the door and helped her father out of the back of the car. They made toward the hospital's automatic front doors, leaving Jenna to trail behind them.

"How old is she—Kasey?"

"Seven," Toby called back as he shuffled along with Dad.

Jenna tried to wrap her mind around the fact that Toby had a daughter—a daughter the same age as Jenna's child would have been if she'd carried to full-term.

But she couldn't process it all. Not right now. It was too much, the emotions that went with what she'd been through during college on top of her worries about her father.

Shaken, she slumped into a chair beside Toby and curled her trembling hands over her stomach as Toby and her father answered the admitting nurse's questions.

Toby ushered Jenna to a waiting area outside the doctor's office. Jenna dragged her feet, her tennis shoes thumping against the polished floor. Mr. Crest had stated he preferred they let him be alone with the hospital staff first, with the promise that he'd call for them once he was ready. Jenna had balked until Toby pressed his hand to the small of her back and steered her out the door. Initially, he was afraid she would fight him, but she'd seemed almost grateful to be redirected.

Now, if only she'd talk.

Jenna rocked in her chair. Her already pale skin had turned ashen. She had her eyes closed tightly and was breathing hard through her nose. Toby dropped into the seat next to hers. Instinctively, he reached to take her hand but stopped himself before he made contact and grabbed the armrest instead.

"Are you okay?"

It was probably a dumb question. Her father was being examined in an emergency room. She'd been sitting in the same waiting room when she learned her mother had passed. This place—the hospital—was woven deeply into both Jenna's and Toby's lives. Not in a good way. Then again, when hospitals were needed, it was hardly ever good news. This was the same emergency room his family had rushed to many times with his brother. Although Toby had usually been sent to the Crests' home, where Mrs. Crest distracted him with apple turnovers and the family included him in their evening board-game tournaments. Toby had spent many nights bunking in their guest room as a child so his parents didn't have to split their time between him and his brother.

"Water." Jenna ran shaky hands down her cheeks. "Can you get water?"

"I'll get you anything you want."

Jenna finally stopped rocking. She tipped her head to the side and studied him for a moment. What did she see? An old friend she trusted? Or still the enemy she'd made him out to be in the orchard an hour ago? Toby feared the latter.

"Water's fine." She looked away.

Toby begged a plastic cup off the ladies at the nurses' station, filled it at the water fountain and then located a vending machine at the end of the hall. Score. It had chocolate-covered peanuts, Jenna's favorite. After getting a pack, he reclaimed his seat and eased the cup into her hands.

She took a long drag of water and then cradled the cup on her lap. "That helped. Thank you." At some point during their dash to the hospital, some of her curls had worked their way out of her ponytail so that they hung around her face. It made her look vulnerable. Protectiveness flooded his heart. Unsure of how she'd respond, he fought the desire to offer her a hug like the old days.

"Here." He passed the chocolate-covered peanuts her way.

Jenna looked up from the cup of water and accepted the bag of treats. "Oh. These are my favorite."

"I know," he said warmly.

"You remembered." Her voice sounded breathless.

"I…" He reached over and tucked her loose curls behind her ear. "I remember almost everything about you."

Her eyebrows pinched together, and she rubbed the heel of her palm against her collarbone.

Toby angled his body toward her. Now was probably the worst time to ask, but he had to know, had to understand why she wasn't happy to see him. Why she'd wanted him off their property. He tried to find a diplomatic way to start. "What are you thinking right now?"

"Sorry." She dropped her hand from her chest. "Sometimes it feels like I'm having a heart attack."

Concern for her dad. Anger at him for taking a job at the orchard. He'd expected one of those answers. Not... heart attack. Wait. Was Jenna ill, too? His gut tightened. "Should I get you a doctor?"

"Please don't. I'm fine."

"Is that a real fine, or like when your dad said he was fine?"

"I don't need a doctor."

"Jenn-nna." He dragged out her name, the way he used to when he was bugging her to tell him something when they were kids.

"I..." She sighed loudly. "You might as well know if you're going to be sticking around..."

"I'm not going anywhere."

"I have anxiety. It's not terrible. And not all the time." She continued, speaking rapidly, almost as if her words might vanish if she didn't get them out fast enough. "But I have attacks—episodes." She shrugged. "Sometimes they're really bad. I'm okay though. Right now. I'm fine."

"You said that." Toby let her words sink in. Jenna hadn't suffered from panic attacks in the past, that he knew of, anyway. Were these new? What caused them? He'd have to do some more research about anxiety before probing further. One thing he understood from having lived with his brother was that where health conditions were concerned, people could unknowingly hurt with poorly phrased questions or assumptions, even when they had good intentions. He wouldn't do that to Jenna.

Jenna set the bag of peanuts in her lap so she could knit her fingers together. "I know it's irrational. I know… It's just, at the time, it's very real." Her gaze latched on to his. "Do you think that's silly?"

"Not at all."

"Seriously?"

"Listen, Jenna, we all have things we struggle with." He took a deep breath. "You clearly already know, but I spiraled into depression after the reality set in that I'd never play professional ball. I had no clue who Toby Holcomb was without that trajectory for my life. Unlike you, I wasn't brave though."

"I'm not brave." She sounded hoarse. "Feeling like the world is collapsing when nothing is actually wrong isn't brave."

"You just told someone. That's brave." Toby rested his elbows on his knees and pressed his hands together. "I was a coward. I didn't tell anyone when I was low." Even himself. He should have known, locked up in his apartment for days at a time. Staying in bed. Not showering. Depression. The mind sure had a strange way of protecting itself…lying. Telling him he was fine. Normal. That how he was acting was how a failure of a man *should* act. He'd lost his dream of being a professional athlete and then tanked the sporting goods business he'd started after that.

Toby Holcomb is a failure.

Toby shook his thoughts away and pressed on. "Instead, like a fool, I self-medicated." He scrubbed his hand over his jaw. *Just say it.* She already knew anyway. "Alcohol. Lots of it, I'm afraid. I'm ashamed to say that it took me almost five years to snap out of it."

Silence. *Say something. Tell me my past doesn't make me a bad person now.*

"What made you snap out of it?" Jenna quietly asked.

God. That was the simple—and complicated—answer. His mother's constant prayers.

"I could really have hurt someone or myself, making poor choices like driving drunk. I thank God for both of those police officers who arrested me. If I hadn't been caught…" He shook his head. "It's more than that though. I was so busy focusing on what I lost—what I felt like was unfairly taken from me—" he tapped the knee that sometimes still gave him trouble, the one that had cost him his career "—that I lost sight of what God put me on this earth to accomplish."

"Football?"

He snorted. "That was something I was good at a long time ago. Something I never used to glorify God. No." He straightened in his seat. He'd never verbalized these thoughts to anyone—not even his parents—but it felt right sharing with Jenna. "I was put on earth for the same reason you were. I'm supposed to love people, Jenna—we're supposed to share God's love with people. No matter what situation I find myself in, I'm supposed to deal with it in a way that points people toward God. That's my purpose."

She pressed her hand into her forehead. "You make it sound like the easiest thing in the world. Dealing with situations that way—as if we're on display for the sake of God."

"Easy? Hardly. But, as Christians, isn't that exactly what our life is supposed to do? At least…I think it is."

Her eyes narrowed. "The old Toby wouldn't have said all this stuff."

He sat up in his chair. Tapped his fingers on the armrest. "The old Toby wasn't a Christian."

"And now?" she whispered.

"I am. Thanks to my mother."

A soft smile lightened Jenna's face. "She never gave up on you."

"I'd long given up on me, but she hadn't. I'm thankful for that. For everyone who pointed me toward God in some way. You included."

Jenna hugged her stomach, her shoulders hunching forward. "I'm not like that anymore. I have a really hard time with some of the things that have happened in my life. I feel like if people knew that I had the anxiety... why I had it..." She shook her head. "If showing people God's love through how I handle my experiences is my purpose in life, then I'm failing."

Toby nudged her arm gently with his elbow. "Good news. I don't think God expects perfection from us. There are all those grace and mercy and forgiveness parts of the Bible to back me up."

Toby looked away. He was a hypocrite, saying things he wanted to believe but wasn't quite sure he really did. He should tell her—tell her that he struggled with wrapping his head around grace and second chances just as much as she seemed to—but the words lodged in his throat.

He glanced back at her. No...he couldn't tell her that he failed at everything. That he was bound to fail in his fresh attempt at a relationship with God. That he'd end up failing her. Again. Like he'd failed her after her mom died. It was impossible to say something like that when she was looking at him for the first time in the old way she used to when they were kids, with her eyes large, lighting up, as if talking together was the best and safest thing in the world.

Jenna relaxed her arms. "That's not the answer I thought you'd have."

Toby swallowed hard. "What did you think I'd say?"

"I thought you'd say you changed for your daughter's sake."

"My—wait—my what?" He jerked his head toward her, trying to read Jenna's face for any signs that she was kidding.

"Kasey…your daughter."

Wait. She thought? No. "Kasey's not my daughter."

"You said earlier that you guessed she was yours." Her brow furrowed. "What does that mean?"

"I was named her guardian in the will."

"Guardian? So who—?"

"You remember Sophia, my cousin, don't you?"

"Sophia died? She was younger than us." Jenna touched his wrist. "Tobe, I'm so sorry." Her hold tightened. "Oh, poor Kasey. Losing her mom so young."

"I hoped you could help her since…" *your mom died when you were young, too.* "I don't know the first thing about taking care of a little girl. When your dad found out, he called and offered the bunkhouse, a job. My parents live in a retirement community, no kids allowed. I'm all Kasey has now. If I hadn't accepted guardianship, they'd have placed her into foster care. I couldn't let that happen." He shook his head.

"You did the right thing." She laid her hand over his for a second, then cupped it back with her other in her lap.

"I can't do it alone though. I don't know what I'm doing." He skirted his gaze to hers. Her deep blue eyes captured his, and he never wanted to look away. They could be friends again. Everything could go back to how it was before. "Will you help me?"

"Of course. However I can."

And just like that, they were a united force. He still needed to get to the bottom of why Jenna had been so upset this morning, but that would come in time.

Chapter Three

Jenna tried to focus on the abstract watercolor in the doctor's office at her father's follow-up appointment the next day. Staring at the strange shapes was easier than looking at her dad or the doctor. Thankfully, Toby had stayed back at the orchard to tend to the work they'd missed yesterday and wouldn't have accomplished today if he hadn't been around. Busy fussing over her father the rest of yesterday, Jenna had missed her opportunity to meet Kasey but hoped to rectify that once she was home from school today.

But after this blow, who knew? A motorized wheelchair. Her father, who used to think nothing of working ten hours a day in the busy season—the man who had taught her to ride horseback, to swim and to race on her bike—was being told it was best for him not to walk on his own going forward.

"You're telling me my father can't walk anymore?" Jenna tried to modulate her voice. It wasn't Dr. Karol's fault—he was a messenger, tasked with delivering bad information. Still, worry simmered through her veins.

"Jenna." Her father's voice held a warning.

But she pressed on. "He fell. Doesn't everyone fall sometimes?" She heard the desperation in her own voice. *Tell me it's all a cruel joke. Tell me Dad will just get better on his own.*

"The type of MS your father has—"

"It's PPMS, I know. I know it's different from normal multiple sclerosis." She didn't mean to be rude, but she'd attended every one of Dad's appointments for the past six months. She had already listened to Dr. Karol talk about Primary Progressive Multiple Sclerosis—PPMS—in detail on many occasions.

Dr. Karol nodded and leaned against the counter. "With primary progressive the legs lose power, and simple tasks, like going out to check the mail, can deplete all of a person's energy."

"And some days it sure does," Dad agreed.

How could he be taking the news so easily?

Jenna clutched the brochure that broke down how much their insurance would cover toward each of their chair options. "But saying he's not allowed to walk… that…that takes away his ability to live." Once people weren't mobile, didn't they get pneumonia? And people could die of pneumonia. That's what had happened to Mom.

The doctor set down his clipboard and opened the small laptop on the counter. "On the contrary. Using a motorized chair, especially with the technology that exists these days, gives back movement and strength. Right now, Richard expends all his energy by noon, just from being mobile in your house. But a chair allows you to store that energy—it gives *back* his life because there are reserves left to spend time with family or go outside.

Think, during harvest your father can come out to the orchard and oversee your work."

Jenna still wasn't convinced as she helped her father into the car and started driving home. Not walking meant accepting defeat. It meant accepting that her father was ill. She wasn't ready for that. Might never be. She tried to repeat what Toby had told her yesterday at the ER. That every situation was a chance to show love—to show God. But her heart had a hard time digesting that. Mom had died so quickly after becoming bedridden. While a motorized chair wasn't the same thing, wasn't it a step in that direction? *Not my dad. I won't let that happen to him, too.*

Her knuckles were turning white on the steering wheel. She eased her grip.

Dad rolled down the window and braced his arm along the frame. Warm September air laced with dampness from Lake Michigan tumbled into the car. "I don't like admitting I need a chair any more than you do, but it seems like the right choice."

Jenna blinked, trying to get a clear view of the road. She needed to be strong for her father. No crying. No falling apart. "We can safety-proof the house. Take away all the rugs and anything that could cause you to trip."

"Jenna."

"And if you want to be part of the harvest, you can ride shotgun in the truck. We take the pickup down the rows anyway. Toby won't mind."

"Jenna."

"And we could—"

"Honeybee, stop. I'm sick." He fisted his hands, but not quickly enough to hide the shaking. From stress. She was causing that. Guilt punched at her heart.

He rested his head against the back of the seat. "My body's failing me. Admitting that is part of being able to move forward and live with my disease."

"Why?" Jenna whispered, so quietly she wasn't sure if her father heard her. A part of her didn't want him to. "Why is God doing this?"

He scrubbed his hand down his face. "He's not *doing this* to me. It's not a punishment. Our bodies fail us because we're mortal. That's all there is to it."

God was perfectly fine with letting people who loved Him suffer? Was it like watching ants on a small anthill? Easy to feel no attachment?

The muscles in her shoulders bunched. She couldn't deal with Dad's train of logic right now. "But they're not letting you walk. Your hands shake all the time. You—"

"It's not a big deal, Jenna."

"Not a big deal? How can you say that? I can't believe—"

"Stop." He drew his hands so they were in his lap, and his gentle blue eyes met hers when she braked at the intersection. "Jenna, sweetheart, the Lord gives and the Lord takes. In all of it let the name of the Lord be praised." He referenced a verse that was written on a plaque that used to hang near the front entrance of their home. Years ago, after Mom's death, Jenna had ripped the plaque down and stuffed it between books on her old childhood bookshelf.

Her father continued. "My hope will remain with my faith, no matter what happens to my body."

No matter what happens to my body. Her throat tightened as if someone had shoved a bundle of itchy wool into her mouth and forced her to swallow. Dad didn't know what those words meant to her, but they still felt like a slap.

"I don't like it. I don't like admitting that you're not a superhero." Her voice shook.

"Every superhero has their foil. I guess PPMS is mine."

"I love you, Dad. You know that, right?"

"I love you, too, sweetheart. I love you very much."

She had to lighten the mood, or else she'd dwell on her thoughts too much and start crying. Besides, she was stressing him out and she didn't want to be the cause of any more issues for him. "So…what you're saying is we should paint the Batman symbol on your motorized chair when they deliver it?"

"Ha! I don't know if I'd go that far. Besides, we heroes like to be more covert." He winked. "If you don't mind."

Her Camry kicked up a cloud of dust as they drove down the driveway. For her father's sake, she parked as close to the house as she could. Just like yesterday, her eyes were drawn to the sagging and worn-down parts of their home. It had once been a beautiful place. Dad used to paint it a brilliant white every summer, even though the orchard demanded so much of his time during that season.

Now the house matched its owner.

"He's changed." Dad's voice dragged her attention away from assessing the house.

Jenna followed the path of his vision to where Toby carried a basket of apples into their barn. He'd been out mending the fence when Jenna conducted her morning perimeter walk. Actually, after they'd arrived home from the ER yesterday afternoon, he must have headed back to her ruined Braeburns, because this morning the baby trees were encircled by plastic orange construction fencing. And two of the ones she'd thought were dead, he'd pruned and retied and was trying to save.

Dad kept talking. "Don't get me wrong. I always liked him. But he's different. I mean that in a good way."

Jenna yanked the keys from the ignition. "I guess."

She didn't want to think of Toby in a good light. That was dangerous. Feeling anything about her old friend would only lead to hurt. They would never be buddies again. The carefree days of lying in the orchard counting stars were gone forever. He wouldn't stay here, not indefinitely. Toby's dreams were bigger than hers. So there was no reason to appreciate him or get attached. Not that she wanted to. Toby was a pest at best and a traitor at worst. She still leaned toward considering him the latter for now.

She rounded the car and helped her father out.

He squeezed her arm. "Whatever happened between the two of you? You used to be inseparable. I figured you'd be over the moon about him coming home, but perhaps I was wrong."

He pretended not to know me. He made fun of your livelihood. Embarrassed me in front of the whole school. And broke my heart in the process. That didn't feel like an appropriate answer, so instead she said, "We both grew up."

"Now, I'm showing my age here, but bear with your old man. Was there ever anything romantic between the two of you?"

Not on Toby's side. Nor would there ever be.

"We're two kids who used to play together. That's all. Nothing more."

"Well, the fact that you're taking a breath belies that. If you're living, there's always more. More to experience. More to know. More to laugh about. More is a gift that should be celebrated every day, honeybee. Toby's back in our lives for a reason. That means he's part of the *more* for both of us."

Yeah, probably *more* pain.

Which was exactly what she was so worried about.

Toby set the crate full of apples on top of the old, rough table that ran the length of one side of the Crests' barn. He scooped an armful of fruit, placed them in the large washbasin sink and started to scrub them.

The Crests weren't farmers, at least not in the normal sense. There were no cows or chickens poking around their ten acres, just apple trees. The barn was separated into three sections—a storage area for equipment, an industrial kitchen area that was set to meet health codes so they could make items to sell and the little storefront in the front of the barn where they sold their goods from the end of September through November, though October was always the busiest time of year.

Perspiration dotted the space between his shoulder blades. He'd forgotten how much manual labor running the orchard could be. How had Mr. Crest managed the past few years? Toby leaned over the sink and cracked the window, letting in a stream of wind. He dragged in a deep breath of air through his nostrils. Sweet notes from the nearby Fuji, Red Delicious and Gravenstein trees flooded his senses. Those smells were home and happiness. Everything he longed for but could never have—not someone like him, not permanently.

Jenna and her mom, along with a team of hired seasonal workers, used to spend all of fall in the kitchen area baking pies, making apple-cider donuts and apple dumplings, loaves and muffins, canning applesauce, and cooking apple butter and jelly. Did Jenna do that all alone now? Did the Crests still run the store at all?

He should have been here. Should have helped them.

A heavy weight settled in his gut.

The Crests weren't his family, not by blood. Even still, he'd spent so many years moping over dreams lost when he could have been of use here. But he could change that now. Toby would be here for them, and he would work hard.

Maybe his life would actually matter. He could finally prove he wasn't a failure.

Okay, that might be asking too much.

Toby dropped more apples into the sink before turning on the faucet. They needed to be scrubbed and chopped; then he could put them in the apple press. Nothing went to waste at the orchard. They always used all the fallen apples to make cider. This would become a daily process once they opened for the season.

The side door creaked, drawing his gaze.

Jenna entered and glanced around. "My dad sent me in here to check on you." She closed the door and moved a few feet closer. "Making cider?"

"I figured it was time for the first batch of the season." He turned off the faucet and pulled the scrub brush off the counter. "You guys still run the store out of the front?"

"We'll open next weekend. The pumpkins should be delivered on Wednesday." She placed a dishtowel over her shoulder, selected a knife from the drawer, gathered a cutting board and joined him by the sink. "You wash, I'll cut."

For a few minutes the only sounds were water sloshing, the rhythmic chops of the knife going through the fleshy apples and a nest of birds outside. When he moved to refill the sink with more apples, Toby snuck another glance at Jenna. Even with her hair tucked back in a ponytail, golden waves framed her face. His eyes ran over her gentle curves. Jenna was beautiful. How had he missed that when he was young?

Even if he had noticed, he'd never have been worthy of her. She was innocent. Pure. He was…he was every mistake in the book, and then some. Someone like him could never deserve someone like Jenna Crest. Not in a million years. Not when he was in high school, and certainly not now.

She stopped cutting and looked over at him. "Need something?" She ran the back of her wrist over her forehead.

He'd been caught staring. Great. Toby cleared his throat as he picked up a few more apples. "How'd your dad's appointment go?"

Her knife stilled over the board. "They said…" She took a breath and started again. "They said he should stop walking." She cut into the apple but then straightened up and rolled her shoulders. "They're making him get a motorized wheelchair."

When Jenna's mom had been unable to walk was when her health had really started to go downhill. Hearing the same news about her father had to have hit Jenna hard. "How bad is he?"

Her forehead wrinkled. She smoothed her fingers over it. "I might as well tell you. I don't really tell anyone this stuff, or what I told you yesterday about my panic attacks, but I guess I will. It's not like you wouldn't figure stuff out, living on our property. Do you know what he has?"

He knew that look. The one that said "Please don't make me explain something I don't want to acknowledge exists." He knew because he'd worn that expression many times himself. He'd spent his childhood pretending to be okay. Pretending his brother's illness and death didn't affect him. Pretending he was the perfect son, athlete, student—anything people wanted him to be— so that he didn't have to answer questions or be honest about what he really felt. Didn't have to tell them he hated it all, the death and the questions and trying to be the son who "deserved" to live. It was all an act. Ben had been a better person than him. Would have been a better man. He would have made his life matter. Toby was sure of that.

Toby knew that in the same way he knew that his own life was a waste.

But thoughts like that wouldn't help Jenna. He needed to find a way to get her to talk more. Engage with him. Stop disliking him.

Toby ran his finger over a splintering crack in the counter. "Primary progressive MS. My mom told me."

"Your mom. Of course." She turned toward him, pressing her hip into the counter. "So how much *do* you know about us?"

He shrugged. His mom was a bit of a talker. Some would call her a gossip.

He wasn't about to admit that he knew it'd taken her six years through correspondence courses to finally achieve her college degree. "You went to college for journalism. Did some freelance writing for a magazine and newspaper out of—" he held up a finger, thinking back over his conversations with his parents "—Grand Rapids. You lived there for a little bit, right?"

Her face clouded and she looked away. "Up until six months ago."

Toby's gut kicked a little. Had she left behind a life she loved back in Grand Rapids? A boyfriend? His chest felt tight. Why did that thought bother him so much?

"Do you miss it?"

She laughed softly. "I was writing a little, but mostly working at the coffee shop below my apartment. Not exactly earthshaking stuff. I was glad to come back. Relieved, actually. Does that make me a bad person?"

He was in a similar place—here because his cousin had passed. Something bad had brought him back, but he'd welcomed any sort of direction in his life. "I hope not, because I was happy to come back here, too."

"I mean, I *had* to come back because my father was sick. And I was happy to have a reason to come back— not happy he's sick, but…does that make sense?" Guilt made her face tense.

A part of him really wanted to open up his arms and offer her a hug, but she wouldn't accept that. At least, he was pretty sure she wouldn't and wasn't brave enough to try without knowing he wouldn't get shot down.

"Completely. You can say anything around me—you know that. We always functioned with the umbrella. What'd we call it?" He squinted, looking at her for the answer.

She sighed, and the tiniest trace of a smile pulled at her lips. "The Umbrella of Grace. Whenever we wanted to say something blunt or hard, we'd pretend to open an umbrella and both stand under it and call it the Umbrella of Grace. We could say whatever we wanted without judgment."

"As long as the umbrella was up." Warmth spread across his chest. How had he forgotten about that? More important, what else had he forgotten when it came to their friendship? He'd blocked most of it out when he left for college, too aware that if he held on to those memories, relived them, it would make him miss things he couldn't have.

But was it possible for him and Jenna to pretend? To act like they did in the old days? As if life could exist simply on the orchard, and they could forget failures and pressure from the outside world? If Toby was excellent at anything, it was pretending.

Toby wiped his hands off on his shirt, then pretended to click an umbrella open and duck under it. "Want to come under here with me?"

She braced her free hand on the counter. "Those days are over. You and I both know that." Her voice shook.

He dropped his hands from his imaginary umbrella. Why didn't she trust him? "Jenna? What happened? What—?"

"I should go check on my dad." She set down her knife and made to leave.

"Hey, stay." Toby caught her arm and gently let his hand slide down to encircle her wrist. "Stay with me."

She focused on where his fingers wrapped around her. For a moment, he thought she was going to shove away from him. Instead she studied his hand as if she were a scientist looking through a microscope at a new life-form.

Toby playfully swung her arm between them. "You okay?"

"That." She licked her lips. "You grabbing me. It should bother me. Why doesn't it bother me?"

He didn't understand what she meant, but he was glad she wasn't upset with him. Toby took a deep breath. "Tell me about your dad. That's where we started before the conversation got derailed."

She twisted to lean against the counter, lightly pulling out of his hold. "He has trouble sleeping. His hands tremble. Six months ago, I didn't know much about MS, and now I feel like I'm an encyclopedia for it."

"I'm sorry." That her dad had an illness. That she was the only family he had, the only one who could shoulder taking care of him long-term. That she'd be alone someday after her dad passed. That her life had been upended by it all.

He was sorry for all of it. But he didn't have to explain. She got it.

"He was diagnosed seven years ago." Her shoulders sagged. "He kept that from me. From everyone. If he had told me when he started feeling bad, I would have left school. I could have left before my sophomore year. Before…" Her gaze sought his, desperate for encouragement. "He was suffering quietly that whole time, and I missed it. How did I miss it?"

"Hey." He clamped his hand on her shoulder and gave a gentle shake. "Don't blame yourself. This isn't your fault. Nothing you did or didn't do caused this or made it worse. You have to believe that, or else questioning it will eat you alive."

"You were so young." She looked at the ground. "With Ben."

Even fifteen years later, he couldn't talk about Ben. Didn't want to. Not even with Jenna.

Toby's arm slacked. "Don't worry about the motorized wheelchair. I get what it means to you…why it's such a hard thing. But I'll help. I'll build a ramp into the house this weekend."

Jenna's eyes went wide. "I didn't even think about that. I should probably move his bedroom downstairs, too."

Toby mapped out their farmhouse in his mind. "Yes, the bedroom can go into his office. That's a great idea."

"And we'll move out the rugs and install some handrails." The first real smile lit up her face. It brought life to her blue eyes, along with the excitement and freedom he was used to seeing there. He'd counted on these expressions from her. She was his beacon of hope, his best friend. Back again. If only for the span of a few heartbeats.

Toby's heart twisted. He'd do anything to get her to smile more around him. "We'll make that place safe for him."

"Thank you." She eased away from the counter. "I really should head in and check on him. I'll talk to him about moving his room downstairs."

"I'll finish the cider and head back out to the orchard." He jerked his head in the direction of the tree line. "It looks like there's going to be a great harvest. You've worked hard here, all on your own. You're a strong woman, Jenna. I hope you know that."

She tossed down the dishrag and muttered, "If only that was true."

He opened his mouth to argue with her, but Jenna headed toward the door. She glanced over her shoulder as she exited. "Bring the cider to dinner. You're welcome to join us around five."

"I'll have Kasey." He pushed his hands into his pockets.

"Kasey's welcome, too. I want to meet her."

"Then we'll be there."

Chapter Four

Jenna dumped chunks of mushrooms into the skillet, followed by a chopped onion and a handful of fresh thyme, pressed garlic, and a dash of salt and pepper. The mixture popped and sizzled in the hot pan, and the earthy aroma from the blend of seasonings made her mouth water. She'd skipped lunch again, hadn't she? Not intentionally. She'd just gotten busy. Jenna rolled her shoulders once. There was way too much to get done before their orchard opened to the public next weekend.

Dad clanked a cup with a plate as he set the table.

She pivoted to watch his movements. How long until he couldn't move at all? Until he lost his sight? Until…?

She had to stop. Those thoughts weren't helpful. More often than not, his gait was jerky and his arms volleyed between the extremes of shaky and stiff, robotic. He tried to hide it. Tried to quell her worries. But watching him made fear claw through her stomach all the same.

Jenna tightened her grip on the skillet's handle.

Not my dad. Don't do this to him. Why is this happening? Why don't You care?

She absently scraped the spatula through the mushrooms. "You don't have to do that," she said to her father.

"I'm perfectly capable of setting a table." He had four more glasses tucked between his arm and chest.

Another clank.

Jenna raised her eyebrows but then took in a deep breath. Even though she wanted to march across the kitchen and pull the cups from his hands, she forced her feet to stay by the oven. It didn't do to argue with him. It just made his face fall, as if he thought she wanted to hurt him. He didn't get it. She was trying to take care of him, make his life easier, and trying to tax him as little as possible so he'd live longer. Why couldn't he see that?

"Jenna, I'm fine."

He moved to set down the next cup and lost hold of it. The glass smacked the edge of the heavy butcher-block-style tabletop, rocketed toward the ground and shattered. He made a late move to try to catch the glass, which sent a second cup down the same path of destruction.

Shards shot around the room like a firecracker going off.

"Oh, dear." Dad gripped the back of the chair and hung his head.

"I'll get it. Don't move." Jenna lurched forward, but smoke curled from the skillet. She needed to take out the mushrooms and put the fillets in, or else dinner would be ruined. But Dad was barefoot and shouldn't be near the glass. He couldn't drop to his knees and clean the mess up either, because it would be too hard for him to get back up off the floor.

She'd have to do it. And figure out how to salvage dinner later.

Although truthfully, all she felt like doing was crying

or screaming. Both at once didn't sound so bad. Watching her father deteriorate piece by piece each day felt as if someone was slowly puncturing the deepest parts of her heart, creating holes where hope and faith leaked out of her life. Drip by drip. Never to return.

The back door opened. Toby's gaze went from the pile of glass on the ground to Jenna's face. He held up a hand to block the child following behind him and then the other one to Jenna so she wouldn't move. He mouthed, "Let me," as he set a jug of fresh cider on the counter. Jenna nodded. She quickly dumped the mushrooms onto a waiting plate but decided to hold off on adding the fillet medallions until the chaos in the kitchen subsided.

Toby smiled at Dad, an understanding passing between them, and then turned toward the small girl. What struck Jenna most was that Kasey looked like a carbon copy of Toby's cousin, Sophia. Her family used to visit the Holcombs every summer. Sophia had even stayed at Jenna's house for a few girls'-night sleepovers. Kasey and her mother shared identical long, dark hair and striking green eyes.

Toby dropped to one knee and placed his hands on her shoulders. "Hey, Kase, I'm going to help Mr. Crest, but first I want you to meet a really good friend of mine." He pointed toward Jenna. "This lady's put up with me since she was younger than you are. Isn't that wild?"

Kasey's chin sank to her chest, and she inched closer to Toby.

He wrapped his arm around her. "It's okay. These are good people. The best. So you don't have to be afraid, all right? You already know Mr. Crest." He gestured toward the man.

Dad waved, and despite the heap of glass at his feet,

a genuine smile warmed his tanned face. "Hey there, pumpkin. I was wondering when you'd come and visit me again."

Toby smiled a thank you and then moved so that he and Kasey were facing Jenna. Jenna got down to one knee, too, and summoned the warmest smile she had.

"This is Jenna. I know you're going to love her." Toby smoothed a hand down Kasey's hair. "Because she's my best friend in the whole world."

Jenna's breath caught, and it suddenly felt like everything in the room had turned and slammed into her chest. *She's my best friend in the whole world.* Why would Toby say something like that? Of course, he was trying to make Kasey feel comfortable around her, Jenna got that. But he shouldn't lie to her. Children were perceptive, more so than most people realized. She'd been older—fifteen—when Mom died, but people had lied to her to try to make her feel better, too. It never worked. Once the grieving kid figured out someone they trusted lied, then they started to question everything. Or learned to pull inward. Neither were good choices.

Kasey's shy gaze met Jenna's and then skittered away, back to Toby's face. "She's really pretty," Kasey whispered to her guardian.

Toby rose to his feet, and his eyes found Jenna's. "You're right. She is."

Jenna opened her mouth to speak, but nothing came out. Why was Toby torturing her? He knew how to say the right things to get what he wanted. That's all he was doing. If only she'd figured that out back when she was a teenager. From the age of nine or ten up until seventeen, Jenna had pictured herself marrying him. Toby had been her hero. Her everything, if she was being honest.

Until he'd made a fool of her, led the school in mocking her and then left.

She couldn't do this. Couldn't live near him. But their lives intertwined now. If she didn't need help on the orchard and with Dad, and if Toby didn't have Kasey and need a place to stay, she'd tell him to leave. Forever. But she *did* need help, and Kasey needed a home. Jenna was stuck.

As if someone had squeezed a corset around her waist, Jenna's lungs felt tight and boxed in. She forced out a breath and held her hand toward Kasey. "I could really use help with dinner."

Toby pressed on the child's back, and she tiptoed over and slipped her fingers into Jenna's. Kasey's hand was so tiny it made Jenna's heart constrict.

"Do you like to cook?" Jenna asked.

"Yes," Kasey answered shyly.

Toby spared them a warm, soft smile and then turned toward her father.

"Hang tight, Mr. Crest. I'll dig you out."

Dad shook his head. "I don't know how it happened. Sorry to burden you all."

Toby crossed to the closet that held all the cleaning supplies. Evidently, even after ten years, he still remembered where they kept everything. "Not at all. Like all boys, I secretly wanted to be a fireman when I was younger, and you're helping me live out my dream." He pretended to push up sleeves, even though he was wearing a crisp navy blue T-shirt. "Commencing rescue mission." He bent over and swept up the majority of the shards before moving onto his hands and knees with damp paper towels. "I think the glassware companies have some sort of conspiracy going. They need us to break their stuff so we buy more." He moved the chair and hunted for pieces under the table.

Dad chuckled. "Of course. They implant them with invisible computer chips, and they're programmed to jump out of our hands after a certain time of owner-ship passes."

"Exactly." Toby crawled toward the pantry and de-posited more glass into the trash can.

Charm might as well have been Toby's middle name, especially where her father was concerned. He'd always had a soft spot for her childhood friend, and their lat-est interaction reminded Jenna why. If she weren't de-termined to dislike Toby, his tender kidding with Dad would have warmed her heart.

Too bad she didn't care about anything having to do with Toby.

Jenna pulled a chair over and then fished a spare apron out of the linen drawer. She looped it over Kasey's head. "I've got red potatoes in the Crock-Pot, and it's just about time to mash them. Think you could do that?"

Kasey nodded. "I'm really good at mashing."

"I thought you might be." Jenna winked at her as she offered Kasey a hand to climb up onto the chair. She unplugged the Crock-Pot and pulled it closer. After she adjusted all the ingredients so they were within Kasey's reach, she explained when to add the butter, cream and seasonings and told her to go ahead and mash away.

Toby finished cleaning the floor and had Dad settled around the same time that Jenna finished the steak me-dallions. She plated the mashed potatoes and meat, cov-ering both with the mushroom cream sauce.

Toby moved Kasey to the table, then sidled up beside

Jenna. "Smells great." His arm brushed against hers. "I forgot what a good cook you are."

She twisted, shoving two plates into his hands. "Try it before you rave about it."

"Don't need to." Toby placed a plate in front of Dad and the other before Kasey. "The smell alone is better than anything I've had in years."

Jenna rinsed off her hands before she brought the other two plates to the table. Toby was in the seat next to hers, his arm hooked over the back of her chair. She had to lean close to set a plate in his spot. He smelled clean—she caught a hint of cedar—and his hair was still a bit damp from a recent shower. She finally dropped down into her seat. They had shared many meals around this table, sitting in the same places, knees nudging whenever they needed to share a secret joke or convey something without her parents noticing.

Well, that wouldn't be happening today. Jenna scooted her chair farther away from him.

Dad reached out his hands, taking one of Kasey's and one of Toby's. "Let's say grace."

Jenna scooped up Kasey's outstretched hand but kept the other one, the one close to Toby, under the table. He simply reached under the table and cupped his hand over hers. His skin was warm, his hand so much bigger than hers. As he held her hand, Toby absently traced his thumb over the back of it. Jenna was having a hard time concentrating. Toby had always possessed the ability to overwhelm her. A part of her wanted to snatch her hand away, but the other part wanted to ask him not to let go. That thought freaked her out more than anything else. She stiffened.

Dad cleared his throat. "Thank You, Lord, for filling

my table again, but not just my table—thank You for filling my life again, too. For my beloved daughter. For bringing back the man I've always considered to be the son of my heart. Thank You, also, for my new friend, Kasey. With these friends here, I feel whole again. Bless this food and bless our conversation, too. Amen."

Jenna yanked her hand away from Toby's and dived into her food, avoiding the questioning look he shot her way. Everyone praised the meal, but it might as well have been cardboard for as much as Jenna tasted. Her thoughts were far away.

Toby's knee bumped hers. It was the "You okay?" nudge. Yes, they'd long ago worked out an intricate type of Morse code, all from nudges. She tucked her leg away from his and dug into her mashed potatoes with more gusto than the spuds called for.

Too bad she and Toby had never worked out a sign for "No, I'm not okay. I'll never be okay, and you're part of the reason why."

Because unlike her father, Jenna had no hope of ever being whole again.

When Jenna and Kasey started to clear the table, they shooed Toby and Mr. Crest out of the kitchen.

"Come on. We're unwanted men at the moment." Jenna's dad rested his hand on Toby's arm. "I haven't had a chance to speak to you much since you got back anyway."

Toby steered the man toward the sitting room located at the front of the house.

The son of my heart. Mr. Crest's words sank into Toby's chest, rattling him. If Jenna's dad really felt that way, then Toby had failed him, too. He was yet another person to add to the Disappointed by Toby Holcomb list.

Why hadn't Toby ever visited? Called? Sent a Christmas card?

He'd been so selfish.

Regret tasted sour at the back of Toby's throat as Mr. Crest shuffled down the hallway beside him.

The second he'd driven under the Crest Orchard sign at the entryway of their property the other day, Toby had actually begun to believe he could do this—be a good guardian for Kasey.

Over the past five months, Toby had struggled to know what to do with Kasey's tears and cries for a mother who would never hug her again. But at the Crest household, he'd always felt like he was someone worthwhile and capable. Ha. Wishful thinking. He was still the same failure of a man he'd been back in Florida. Really, the one he'd always been, even here in Goose Harbor. The Crests had just always looked past that. They had cared without expecting anything of him. He'd spent every summer of his childhood zigzagging through the lanes of trees with Jenna. They'd built forts and dreamed of what life would be like when they grew up. She'd held his hand during his brother's funeral.

Toby swallowed past the lump in his throat.

A lot of time had passed since then, and all of the dreams they'd pored over in their youth hadn't come to fruition. Not one. Toby wasn't a national football star, Jenna wasn't a bestselling author and neither was happily married with kids, as they'd assumed they'd both be by now.

Although, he had a seven-year-old child he was responsible for, so maybe he could start rewriting his future. Maybe that was what God was doing—writing a new chapter in his life by bringing him back to the place where all his hopes had once taken root. And boy, did he need a new chapter. He couldn't afford to be a failure now, not with Kasey depending on him.

Toby took the wing-backed chair off to the side of where Mr. Crest sat. Other than the new-looking couch along the back wall, their front room looked the same as it had been the last time he'd been here.

Jenna's dad picked up the Bible resting on the small table between them. "How are you, son? And I don't mean today. Your parents have kept me up to speed on most things, but I want to know where you stand with God these days."

In an effort to hide his smile, Toby smoothed his hand over his mouth. Mr. Crest had never been one to beat around the bush. For that, he deserved an honest answer. No matter how raw it left Toby.

"After my injury—" Toby cleared his throat. "After my life didn't go as planned, I went down the wrong path. I'm ashamed to say that it took me longer than it should have to get back on track." *Just own up to your mistakes. Mr. Crest already knows them.* "My second drunk-driving arrest was the shock I needed to clean up my life. I've been sober for two years now. In that time I started attending church with my parents and have been reading through the Bible. I'm a Christian, if that's what you're asking."

Mr. Crest hugged his Bible. "You say your life didn't go as planned—well, that seems to be a running theme for everyone on this earth. I didn't plan to lose my ability to run this place due to illness, and yet here I am." He tapped the Bible. "But I find I'm in good company. Do you know not one person in this book had their life go according to their own plans? Not one, son. Think about that." He fanned the pages so they made a slight whooshing sound. "Yet God used them. Sometimes He gave them a greater plan, and sometimes the plan for their life was so different from their own that they fought tooth and nail against God. Letting go of our human plans is the first step to living by faith. I'm proud of you, Toby."

Uncomfortable with the man's high regard for him, Toby shuffled his feet. "It would have been better if I hadn't wasted a handful of years being messed up though."

"Maybe so, but maybe not. You're the man you are now because of those things. If you hadn't been injured at that final game, you'd be playing football on the national scene right now—how would that have prepared you for your role as guardian?"

Who knew? If Toby had achieved his dream, the one that had been within his grasp until the career-ending tear in his knee, he definitely wouldn't have been able to drop everything and move to take care of Kasey. That much was true.

Toby rested his elbows on his knees and leaned forward, hands together. "Mr. Crest?"

"It's Rich."

He shook his head. "I'll never be able to call you by your first name." Toby looked down at his hands. "With all you're going through, it's just…"

"What is it?"

"It doesn't seem like you're afraid of anything. How do you do that?"

Mr. Crest set his Bible back on the table. "I have fears. Everyone does."

"What are you most afraid of?" Toby asked quietly.

"Leaving Jenna all alone."

Not dying? Not losing his purpose? Toby kept his eyes on the intricate pattern that spanned the edges of the Oriental rug beneath them. Emotion grabbed him, lodging in his throat as a slow burn simmered in his gut. The thought of Jenna completely alone—no family—left him feeling ill.

Toby's mouth went dry. "Sir, you don't have to worry about that. I promise she won't be alone."

Mr. Crest cocked his head. "You don't know what you're saying."

"Yes, yes, I do." Toby straightened up, hooked his ankle on his knee and rested back against the chair. "I have nowhere else to go. I can't live at my parents' retirement community. I tried to start a business and had to close the doors within a year. I…" He shrugged. "This is the only place I've ever fit. I'll stay here and take care of her, if she'll let me."

"It's a nice thought." Sadness clouded Mr. Crest's eyes. "But outside of one circumstance, it's an impossible promise to keep."

"You don't think I'll do it?"

"Oh, I think you're serious, but, son, what would you do if Jenna fell in love with someone? Then what? You two can't play house here like you used to when you were knee-high." He wore a far-off gaze, as if he was picturing five-year-old Jenna and Toby playing blocks together in the very same room. "I want love for Jenna, real, true love. Not a brother-type figure."

"Well, sure." Toby coughed. "I mean, if there was someone…if a guy came along…of course I'd get out of the way." The words had been forced out, and Toby wasn't sure if they were true. He'd been back for only a few days and Jenna was all bristles and thorns toward him, but still, the thought of handing her over to someone else's care didn't sit well. Jenna was a vital part of almost all of his good memories, and her smiles, her encouragement, were the only happy spot in the midst of his bad memories.

Mr. Crest shifted in his seat. "And if you find someone to marry, what becomes of Jenna?"

Toby barked out a laugh before he could rein it in. "That's not going to happen. Marriage isn't for me."

The man's eyebrows rose slowly. "You want me to rewind the conversation to when we both agreed that the Lord wants us to let go of our plans?"

Toby sprang to his feet. "Believe me. I'm not getting married. It's not something I want."

Jenna's dad pursed his lips and studied Toby. Then he gently asked, "And why not, son?"

Because Toby would no doubt fail at that, too.

He just shrugged.

Mr. Crest leaned on his armrest. "What if one of you falls in love with the other, but the other doesn't feel the same way?"

"Well, like I said, I have no interest in dating. And seeing as I'm pretty sure Jenna hates me—" Toby scratched the back of his head "—I don't foresee that being an issue."

Her father nodded. "I've noticed her glares in your direction. Do you know why?"

"No clue."

"Why don't you ask her?"

Toby sighed. Could it really be that easy?

Mr. Crest folded his hands in his lap. "Go into that

kitchen for me and send Kasey in here. I promised I'd teach her to play chess."

Toby shook his head as he walked into the hallway. Leave it to Mr. Crest to immediately set Jenna and Toby up to be alone. Well, fine. Toby would corner her and try to get to the bottom of her anger.

Chapter Five

The air felt heavy and stuffy inside the church. It was mid-September. They should still have the air-conditioning running. Was it broken? Not likely, as the building was only a year old.

Jenna bunched the fabric of her shirt in her fist and fanned it, trying to cool down.

The young pastor of Goose Harbor Community Church—Jacob Song—bowed his head for the final prayer, and Jenna tried to focus, but that seemed to be an effort in futility recently.

Yup, pinpointed to the moment Toby returned to Goose Harbor.

She shifted in her seat and stared at the palms of her hands. Breathe. In and out. There. *Not so hard, is it?* But it was. When her mind started spinning, when her chest started to feel compressed, it was.

Air. She needed some fresh air and space away from a roomful of people. Sure, she loved the members of her church and Pastor Song was an excellent preacher, but anxiety was unpredictable that way.

Jenna scooted away from Dad and slipped out of the

pew. Toby was seated on his other side, so he'd be there if Dad needed help moving around after the service, and if Toby abandoned her father, Dad usually sat and read his Bible while he waited for Jenna to return. Thankfully, they always sat toward the back. She easily made it out of the sanctuary, crossed the lobby and pressed through the front doors all within the span of a minute.

Knees trembling, she sank down onto the front steps and counted backward from ten. Why was she freaking out? What had set it off this time? She wanted to determine the cause so she could take measures against it happening again. That was the only way she'd found she could control the attacks.

Ha. There was no controlling them. That was a myth. But she could attempt to avoid triggers.

Although, sometimes—like now—she couldn't nail down a reason.

Dampness coated the wind, an ever-present reminder of Lake Michigan's proximity. A fat bee lazily tested each of the flowers that lined the path along the edge of the building.

Toby had tried to corner her again this morning, asking if she was willing to talk about the past. He'd done that three times since the first night he and Kasey had joined them for dinner. Would it become a daily battle with him? Each time, she'd babbled about being stressed over the condition of the house and orchard in the wake of the opening next weekend, which had redirected the conversation. But apparently Toby wasn't going to give up easily.

The door behind her clicked, making Jenna sit up and spin around.

Cradling her newborn in her arms, her friend Paige

Beck ducked through the doors and smiled at her. "I was rocking him in the new-mothers' room and saw you walk past," she whispered as she sat down beside Jenna. "I could use adult conversation." She bumped her shoulder into Jenna's.

Paige had moved to Goose Harbor only a few years ago, but the tall blonde with her kind spirit had quickly found her way into the hearts of all the residents. In a whirlwind romance, she'd married lifelong resident Caleb Beck. The two were a perfect couple. With Caleb's heart of gold and Paige's ability to make everyone feel loved, they had a huge impact on the students they taught at the high school. Jenna hadn't seen either one of them stop smiling since the birth of their son.

Jenna wrapped her arm around her friend's waist so she could lean close for a good look at baby Noah. He had his eyes closed, but he reached his little fist up out of his blanket in a big yawn. Emotions piled up against Jenna's heart. She'd always wanted a family—children of her own—but with no plans to ever date again or get married it was a dream she'd given up on. After Dad passed, she'd be all alone.

She choked down her personal pain and smiled at her friend. "Oh, Paige, I know I've said it before, but he's perfect. I'm so happy for you and Caleb."

Paige ran her fingers over Noah's dark, downy hair. "He's handsome. Like his daddy."

"How old is he now?"

"Just over two months."

"My offer to watch him whenever you want still stands."

Paige sighed. "Oh, don't worry. I plan to take you up on that offer and then some. Especially when Kellen and

Maggie take off on their honeymoon here soon. Usually either Shelby or Maggie watches him when I need a nap or need to, you know, shower. Exciting things like that."

Jenna touched Noah's soft fisted hand. "Well, I'm serious."

"I know." Paige tucked the baby so his head rested on her shoulder. She studied Jenna for a moment. "Sometimes I fear you're too serious for your own good."

Paige had a way of zeroing in on exactly what someone needed to talk about—no matter if they wanted to have the talk or not. With Paige's sweet manner, it was impossible to tell her no or to brush off her questions. She was tricky that way.

So Jenna hedged with "What do you mean?"

"You're so young. You should be enjoying life."

"I enjoy life."

Paige's brow creased. "Do you?"

Jenna sighed and scrubbed her hand down her face. "I don't know. There's a lot I'm responsible for. The orchard and my dad. And I've never been someone who wanted to go out and party or anything like that. That's not my idea of a good time."

And when she had taken chances and tried to live, as Paige put it, she'd ended up burned. It had ruined her life.

"Oh, I don't think you have to party to have a good time." Paige rolled her eyes. "Look at me and Caleb. We're the total opposite of party animals, but we love every minute of our lives. That's what I'm talking about."

Jenna pinned her hands between her knees. "I guess I'm a boring person."

"Hardly." Paige rocked a little when Noah made a

small noise. "What about this man I keep hearing about. It's Toby, right?"

"How do you know about Toby?" Paige hadn't been around during high school. She wasn't a Goose Harbor lifer. Beyond the awards and records bearing his name that were still tucked in the trophy case at the high school, Paige had no reason to know who Toby Holcomb was.

"Well, one, word gets around fast in this town. But two, that man's called Caleb a couple of times this week. They're working on a project together."

Project? She hadn't heard Toby mention a project. But something else seemed more important. "I didn't even know Caleb and Toby were friends."

"Caleb's older." Paige nodded. "But I guess they both played on the varsity football team together back in the day."

Noise filtered through the front doors. People were mingling in the lobby. The service had let out, and soon everyone would be tromping past where the women sat.

Jenna glanced over her shoulder, making sure no one was nearby. "Right. Toby made varsity his freshman year."

"Were you two close?"

Jenna hugged her stomach. "He was my best friend." For a long time, her only friend.

Paige squeezed her arm. "How wonderful to have him back, then."

"No. It's not wonderful at all." Jenna shook her head. Hugged herself tighter. "We had a falling out. Now it's just uncomfortable. He tries to act like nothing has changed, and I don't know what to do with that."

"He hurt you a lot, didn't he?"

Jenna shrugged.

"You're still in love with him." Paige said it like it was a fact. As if she knew.

Which was impossible. Jenna didn't even know how she felt about Toby. It changed from minute to minute.

"Still? But I've never told anyone how I used to feel about him."

"Relax." Paige adjusted Noah so he was cradled in her arms again. "I'm a woman. That's all I needed in order to see the truth. I can hear what you're not saying."

Jenna relaxed her arms and rolled her shoulders. "I have no desire to be friends with him again."

"After I found out my fiancé cheated on me, I never wanted to trust a man again. I'd been let down by every man I'd dated before him. Then I found out my father had cheated on my mother multiple times during the course of their marriage. I told myself I would never open my heart to that possibility."

"Then Caleb happened."

"Wrong. Then God happened." She tucked the brown blanket more snug around her baby. "I had to trust that God could heal me and that He wouldn't hurt me before I was willing to be in a relationship with a man. I almost missed out on the love I have with Caleb because I was so stubborn about protecting my heart."

Sure, but God cared about Paige. He'd protected her from her uncaring fiancé and brought her a man like Caleb. It was very different from Jenna's experiences. God had taken Jenna's mother away when she was fifteen. God allowed her father to be stricken with a debilitating and hopeless illness. And God hadn't protected Jenna when she had needed Him most. Not with Ross... not even when she cried out to Him. The bottom line was God didn't care about her. Maybe He cared about other people, but not Jenna Crest.

Paige gave a quiet, small laugh. "I tried to protect my heart from God. Which is madness. His hands are the only safe place. Don't get me wrong. I love my husband. Caleb's the best man I have ever known. But a little secret here—Caleb's not perfect." Paige's smile was full of joy. "Just because I'm married to a good and honorable man doesn't mean my heart will never hurt again. No one can be guaranteed that."

"Then why open yourself up at all?"

"Because of the joy I have with Caleb, and now this little man, too." She patted Noah. "That's worth any hurt I'll ever have to face."

The front door opened, and a flood of people started to exit. They filed past Paige and Jenna. A couple people whispered hellos or cooed at sleeping Noah.

Jenna lowered her voice, hoping to end the conversation before anyone overheard them. "Fine, but you're not with the man who hurt you. It's still different."

"From everything Caleb's told me, it sounds like Toby's a good guy. But it's not him, is it? Not really?"

"Oh." Jenna huffed. "It's completely him."

"No." Paige narrowed her eyes. "It's God you don't trust."

She'd thrown a zinger right to the heart. And wow, it hurt.

Jenna rocked her feet to the sides and stared down at the pavement. "I don't really want to talk about it."

Caleb passed them on the steps and then turned around so he was eye level with his wife. He reached out to relieve her of Noah. "Morning, Jenna."

She smiled a greeting, found her feet and brushed off the back of her dress.

Paige grabbed on to Caleb's free hand, and he helped her stand. She threaded her hand through the loop in his arm and then faced Jenna again. "No one's making you, but if you ever want to talk, I'm here. I'm on maternity leave, and this guy—" she pointed at Noah "—he doesn't sleep through the night, so if you want to talk at two in the morning, just call. Will you promise to keep one thing in mind for me though?"

"Sure."

"Talking about stuff doesn't mean you're losing faith—it actually means you're brave enough to face it," Paige said.

"Believe her." Caleb beamed at his wife. "This woman knows all. She calls me on my stuff all the time."

They all laughed, but watching the way Caleb and Paige interacted made Jenna's throat feel raw. The couple had everything she ever wanted. Love. A child. Mutual respect. The support of a best friend.

"Paige can't join us, but I'll see you later." Caleb waved and steered his little family toward their car.

See you later? What on earth was Caleb talking about?

Toby peeked over to where Jenna sat in the passenger seat of his SUV. They'd taken to driving his vehicle whenever the four of them traveled together because Kasey's booster seat was set up in his backseat. Not that it would take more than two minutes to move it into Jenna's car, but what they were doing now worked well. Toby and Jenna rode in the front, and her dad and Kasey rode together in the back—they felt like a family.

If only Jenna weren't acting like an angry stepcousin. Her dress was some shade of pink or orange. Did women call that *coral*? When she'd walked down the steps of her house that morning to meet him and Kasey on the porch, Toby's mouth had gone dry. No one had ever taken his breath away, but now Jenna held that distinction. The dress hugged her torso and then went out from the waist to her knees. She wore small heels, and loose curls ran freely down her back. A pop of a light red color on her lips completed the look. Toby had edged closer to her when he noticed a couple guys checking her out as they had walked into church. It took everything in him not to wrestle her father—figuratively speaking— for the right to sit next to her in the pew.

After church they drove to Happy Tails Dog Sanctuary, located on the edge of the Dunes State Park. One of Jenna's friends, Shelby, ran the place with her fireman boyfriend, Joel. Mr. Crest had reached out to Shelby to set up a time for him and Kasey to go visit and play with the dogs. After they'd dropped off her dad and Kasey, silence pulsed between Toby and Jenna.

Toby turned down the music. "I'm sorry I was late coming out of church. Kasey introduced me to her teacher, who goes there, too. I wanted to catch her anyway and see how Kasey did during her first week."

Apparently, Kasey had pulled inward at school. It was understandable, considering all the child had been through in the past five months. She'd lost her mother— the only family she'd known—then met and was immediately handed over to her new guardian and had left her home and all her belongings and friends to move to Goose Harbor. Being reserved now was pretty much a given for her. Her teacher had promised to keep Toby up to date on any changes in her behavior or motivation levels.

Jenna smoothed nonexistent wrinkles from her dress. "Who's her teacher?"

Toby tapped the steering wheel, thinking. "Miss Vincent."

"Gotcha. That's Leah. She's cute."

Miss Vincent had been petite. Did she have dark hair? He couldn't remember anything else beyond that. He'd spent the conversation focused on Kasey, who was hanging from his arm asking about the puppies. "I guess."

"She's single," Jenna offered.

"So are you." At least, he was fairly certain she was. Now was her opportunity to set him straight if she wasn't. She rolled her shoulders and flipped her hair behind her, leaving a wake of lavender in the air that twisted his heart. She still smelled like the same lotion she'd used in high school.

She'd given no answer. That was good. Right? He cleared his throat. "I saw you talking with Paige."

Jenna rubbed her thumb back and forth along her wrist. "Do you think God cares about you?"

Toby's heart stalled for a second. Was she trying to pick a fight with him, or was it a real question? Was she hinting at the fact that she thought he wasn't a good Christian? He wouldn't blame her if she doubted his sincerity. Jenna of all people knew how good he was at faking his way through life. She was easily the only person in the world who had ever known the real Toby Holcomb, the one who hid behind the image of star athlete and always-happy, outgoing popular guy.

Her question was open and honest. Oh, she wanted him to actually answer that.

Do you think God cares about you? Toby had given Him no reason to.

Holding the wheel with one hand, he used the other to knead a muscle in the back of his neck. "Where's this coming from?"

"I just…" She yanked a bracelet off her wrist and worked it around in her hand. "Does He care about each one of us, as individuals? Or is it more that He cares about humanity? Or maybe some people more than others?"

Toby turned down the country road that took them inland, farther from Lake Michigan. The lanes narrowed and trees cropped up on either side of the road. At night it became dangerous with deer crossing, among other things. The road started at almost a blind curve, with forest on either side. As a teen, he'd spun out a few times there in the winter. He'd always hated that part of the road.

He tried to work through Jenna's questions, turning them over in his head to figure out what she was really asking. Jenna had a tendency of rambling when she was unsure or feeling insecure. The fact that she'd done that with him didn't go unnoticed. She was warming to him on some level, even if she wouldn't talk about the past. Seeking his opinion on something spiritual meant she had at least an ounce of trust in him. He'd take what he could get.

What was she really getting at? *Does God care about me?*

Toby adjusted his hold on the wheel to free up his right hand. Taking a risk, he reached over and grasped her hand. "God cares about you, Jenna. I know that's true."

She looked down at their hands but didn't pull away. "I want to believe that's true," she whispered.

Her forlorn tone found soft soil in his heart and twisted, slicing him open inside. Jenna didn't believe God cared about her. How could she not see how special she was? It took all of his self-control not to jerk his vehicle to the side of the road, toss it into Park and pull her into his arms. Hold her until she believed that she was precious and worth cherishing. Get to the bottom of whatever had made her think otherwise.

Forcing his attention to stay on the road, he took a deep breath. "Why don't you believe it?"

"God never rose to protect me against anything that's happened. Not with my mom, or now with my dad, or other times." Her voice shook. Toby squeezed her hand, offering silent encouragement. "I've cried out to Him so many times and everything—really bad stuff—still happened."

Toby glanced her way, but her gaze dropped before he could make eye contact. A sense of unease churned in his stomach. He knew about her parents, but what "really bad stuff" had happened to Jenna?

They turned down the long gravel driveway that belonged to Crest Orchard, and Jenna yanked her hand away from his. She couldn't yet see his surprise, but he prayed she would be happy with all he'd planned.

Give me the words to say.

"God cares about you. More than that, He loves you, Jenna. You can't question that. You've lived a life that…" He swallowed hard. "You have no reason to question why God would care about you." Unlike Toby, who had partied during high school, burned his way through several girlfriends in college and then fallen into a self-medicating depression. He'd constantly failed God. *That* kind of life made a man question if God could care about him.

"No reason?" She bristled. Her fingers flexed. "You have no idea what you're talking about."

"I know you." He kept his voice soft, soothing. "You've lived an honorable life. You do everything right. You—"

"You don't know me at all." She yanked her hand away from his.

They started to round the bend in the driveway where the tree line opened up to show the farmhouse. A bus, a few pickup trucks and a team of thirty or forty guys came into view. It looked like they'd already started working on the house.

Jenna unsnapped her seat belt and leaned forward, hands braced on the dashboard. She looked at the people swarming her orchard and then at Toby, then back at the crowd. "Who are they? What are they doing? I don't understand."

Toby pulled the keys out of the ignition and jangled them in a nervous motion. *Please don't bite my head off for planning this behind your back.* "You said you were worried about the house and grounds being ready on time. Your dad knows this is happening. Everything's being done with his permission."

Caleb and a few other men were directing the teens in their tasks—the entire high school football team, from the looks of it. Toby recognized Evan Daniels, another Goose Harbor lifer. Evan ran a woodworking business, volunteered with the youth group and was known to be handy. There were two power washers going, tarps already down and at least twenty teenagers scraping old paint off the house's exterior. Another group could be seen fixing up the front of the country storefront attached to the barn. Toby would have them clean inside there, too.

She swiveled and grabbed his forearm. "You did this? How? Why?"

He didn't move. It was the first time Jenna had initiated physical contact with him, and he wasn't about to ruin the moment. "I worked out a deal with Caleb for the whole football team to give some volunteer labor to help us get everything ready on time."

She leaned closer, her eyes wide, giddy. He saw a glimmer of his old best friend. "What type of deal?"

He ran his tongue over the back of his teeth and then sighed. "It doesn't matter."

The pressure in her fingertips doubled. "I can't afford to pay all these people."

"Ah, see, that's the beauty of the word *volunteer.*"

"Tobe." She shook his arm. "Tell me. What did you promise them?"

She'd find out anyway. "Well, you're looking at the new assistant coach for the high school. I'm going to teach some special clinics, too." All for free, for the entire season. But she didn't need to know that part.

"Thank you. Really. This is… Thank you." She smiled at him, a real, wonderful, heart-crushing smile, and then let go of his arm and exited his SUV.

Toby hung on to the steering wheel, gathering his bearings. Every interaction with his childhood best friend made his heart drum hard against his ribs. What was happening to him? He hadn't felt like this since… since he'd left town ten years ago. Since he'd left her.

He had to win back her good favor. He wanted to *deserve* that smile. He missed her friendship, more than he'd ever realized.

Chapter Six

Between yesterday, when the football team had worked at the orchard for seven hours, and today, when they'd returned after school to paint the house, bunkhouse and barn, Crest Orchard looked like a completely different place.

Jenna pulled back the lace curtain that hung over the kitchen sink to spy on Toby. He was out on the porch that wrapped around the house, talking with Evan Daniels. All the other workers had left for the night. She dropped the curtain and headed toward the front sitting room. Peeking around the corner, she spotted her father sitting on the couch watching a historical special with a zonked-out Kasey curled against his side.

Dad held a finger to his lips. "The little thing's all tuckered out. She's had a lot of excitement in the last few days. Let's let her rest."

Jenna nodded as she bit back a smile. Sure, Kasey was overtired, but her early bedtime probably also had something to do with the logical sugar crash that had accompanied the copious amount of ice cream she'd consumed today. Dad had been indulgent. Jenna knew he loved spending time with his new little buddy. Kasey already treated him like a grandfather.

The monotone speaker on the documentary began to list off all the programs encompassed in FDR's New Deal. Jenna couldn't blame Kasey for falling asleep during one of Dad's shows. As a child, Jenna had done the same. Her dad had a fascination with biographies.

"Need anything?" Jenna whispered.

"Thank Toby again for me, will you?"

She pressed her hands into the solid doorframe behind her. "I will." She paused, not sure how to continue. She'd wanted to broach the money topic with him since returning but had never found a delicate way to do so. "Hey, Dad?"

"What's on your heart, honeybee?"

"I know the labor was free, but I need you to be upfront with me about our financial situation. How much does the orchard have to make in the next two months in order to afford all these improvements?"

He yawned, settling into the couch a little deeper. "We're not in debt for any of it."

Jenna calculated the supplies needed to fix parts of their house and roof, the cost of the wood they'd used to build ramps into both the house and the barn. Paint, rental equipment, the catered food that had shown up for lunch and dinner yesterday and dinner tonight. She hadn't ordered that stuff, but food to feed fifty people—most of them teenage athletes—didn't run cheap. Wood alone was expensive.

"How much did all of it cost?"

"Well, this is tricky." Dad shifted. "I promised not to say."

"Promised? Promised who?" Jenna rocked forward. "Toby?"

Kasey let out a little moan and flipped so she was facing the back of the couch.

"Enough of that." Dad bunched up his mouth. "Keep your voice down."

"Fine." She put her hands up in surrender. She wasn't going to get any more information out of him. Not tonight, at least. "Can I bring you anything? Tea? Cider?"

He shook his head and adjusted the blanket draped around Kasey. Good thing they had Toby around to carry Kasey to her bed later. The girl was tiny but still more weight than Jenna could lift and haul outside and into the bunkhouse. Come to think of it, the bunkhouse had only one bedroom. If Toby gave Kasey the bedroom, where was he sleeping?

Jenna turned and sagged against the wall in the hallway, where Dad couldn't see her. *Thank You, God, for giving him this special bond with Kasey. For giving them each other. Especially since I don't think he'll ever have a grandchild.*

A sharp stab, followed by a familiar ache, spread through Jenna's chest. She wouldn't let herself dwell on it. After the miscarriage she had suffered during college, she'd decided that the only way to protect herself from experiencing that level of pain was to never enter into a relationship again. Beyond that, men had hurt her. Ross, her college boyfriend, should be in jail for the pain he'd caused her.

Her feet heavy as concrete, she forced herself to shuffle back to the kitchen. Dad had asked her to thank Toby again, so she would. Besides, if she was stuck with her old friend for the long term, she had to start talking to him. They could be cordial and keep all conversation on the surface.

She and Toby had spent the last two days brushing shoulders as they scrapped the house, worked on the yard and painted side by side. With aggravating precision, he seemed to be aware of what she needed at all times, from handing her a bottle of water right when she started feeling thirsty to setting up the country store exactly how she always did without her explaining anything. Moreover, he'd taken it upon himself to check on her father every hour and make slight accommodations to tasks so that Dad could help, too.

Before sunset, the four of them had stood together outside the house and surveyed all that had been accomplished. Dad had looked so proud. Their house—gleaming white with red painted trim, flowers hanging from all the baskets on the railing of the porch and pumpkins lining the steps—hadn't looked that good since before Mom passed away.

What did Toby stand to gain by treating the Crests with such kindness? Was it only that he felt indebted to her father? Or something else? What if he planned to leave them high and dry like he'd done in the past? Either way, Jenna needed to find out.

She glanced out the window again. He was still visiting with Evan. He and Toby were making big hand gestures. Football talk or something equally manly, no doubt, but she planned to catch him when Evan left.

Remembering that caramel cider was one of Toby's favorite drinks, Jenna pulled ingredients from the cupboard. While she and Toby might be at odds, Mom had instilled a deep respect for good manners before she died. After all the extra work he'd poured into the orchard so far, offering him a small bit of refreshment was the least she could do.

She added equal parts brown and white sugar to a pan with water and stirred the mixture until it rose to a slow boil. The scent of the hot sugar water filled the room with a light sweetness. After she removed the mixture from the heat, she measured cinnamon and stirred until it was blended. Then she poured fresh cider over the homemade cinnamon dolce syrup and set the pan on the burner again, stirring the mixture constantly. She closed her eyes for a moment, breathing in the smell of mulled cider—it smelled like fall, harvest, apples, home, Mom. Toby fit somewhere in there, too, didn't he?

Don't think about that.

Over the last few days, she might have stopped wishing he would disappear from her life, but that didn't mean she wanted anything beyond a working relationship with him. At best, Toby was a hired hand who did good work, and she wanted to know what his angle was in all of this. End of story.

Once a few minutes had passed, she turned off the burner, ladled the caramel cider into two mugs and then dug whipped cream and caramel syrup out of the fridge to top off the drinks. She even took the extra couple of seconds to make a fancy design with the syrup. With a cup in each hand, she used her foot to open the back door and then stepped outside.

Evan spotted her first and offered a one-hundred-watt smile. He was a few years older than her, and Jenna had to admit that Evan was awfully handsome. His swooping dark hair looked like something out of a shampoo advertisement, and he wore a tool belt as if it were a trendy fashion accessory. If one of the cable home-improvement networks ever stumbled upon him, they'd offer a contract on the spot, and women all over the country would lose their hearts after the first episode. Evan had a reputation in town as a horrible flirt, but thankfully, he'd never tried to flirt with Jenna, so they were able to be friendly acquaintances.

"Can I interest either of you in hot cider?" She crossed toward the back stairs where the two men huddled.

Evan held up a hand. "Man, that smells so good, but I should head home. My alarm clock sounds early. But you two enjoy." He pointed at Toby. "Think about what I said."

Toby uncrossed his arms and reached out to ease a mug from Jenna's hand. "Will do."

Evan bid goodbye and shrugged off her praise for all his hard work. "It's what neighbors do." He headed for his car, and his headlights blinded them temporarily as he backed down the driveway.

"Good guy." Toby tipped his mug to indicate where Evan had left.

"He really is." Jenna dropped onto the large bench swing hanging from the porch. Someone had replaced the old, creaky chains in the course of the work during the last few days, but the wood still groaned as she set it into motion.

"May I?" Toby pointed at the space beside her.

Jenna caught her toes on the ground, stopping the swing long enough for him to take his seat. They didn't set it rocking right away. Instead Toby wrapped an arm across the back of the chair behind her and cupped his mug in his other hand. Despite the fact that he wasn't touching her, Jenna's neck and shoulders blazed as if he were. He was so near, and he smelled like a delicious mix of cedar and mulled cider and sweat.

Memories from years ago hit her with the force of a punch to the jaw.

In the past, the two of them had spent many evenings here. He would arrive home, dog tired from football practice, but he'd still come over so Jenna could tell him stories. She'd store up things to share with him all day long, and he'd listen as she rattled on, some nights for hours. When she felt brave, she would lay her head on his shoulder, praying that they could stay like that forever.

Jenna had imagined them sharing their first kiss there, cuddled together under the stars. She'd even gone so far as to wonder if he'd propose on the bench. Or whether he would favor the tree house in the forest beyond the orchard, where they had forged their friendship early on in childhood, pretending to be jungle adventurers together, discovering new lands.

Neither, apparently. Because Toby had never thought of her that way, a realization that still stung. The world could be so cruel. He was the only man she had ever loved. And the only man she ever would. She knew that for sure because she was never going to open her heart up to that magnitude of pain again.

He took a swig from his mug and moaned. "Wow, that's good. Your mom's recipe, right?" Another sip. "The last time I had this…" His voice dropped.

Yeah, they both knew. There was no reason to speak about it. Last time he'd tried to talk to her, and she'd ended up prying the mug from his hands, dumping the drink in the yard and telling him not to come back.

Being out here with him, reliving an old tradition… What a horrible idea.

She inched away from the shelter of his warmth on the bench, then sprang from her seat and set her mug down on the little table under the window.

"Anyway, my dad said to tell you thanks again for all you've done for us." She rolled her shoulders. Paced away from him. "You've done more in a week than I was able to accomplish in the past six months."

"Jenna." His voice held a warning. Hearing her being self-deprecating had never sat well with him.

She backed up so she could lean against the side of the house, a good distance away from him. Sweet, wonderful distance. That was better. Safer. "I wanted to thank you, too. I have a feeling you did more to make this happen than you're letting on." Like financing everything. "It makes me wonder why."

His brow scrunched. "I care about this place. I care about—"

"Toby, don't. Come on. Don't pull that with me."

"Pull what?" He rocked forward, his muscles coiled as if he were back on the football field at the start of a play. Ready for action. "I'm not pulling anything. I care about you and your dad, and about the orchard. I always have. You guys are a second family to me."

Lies. All lies.

"Don't say stuff you don't mean."

He balanced his mug on the edge of the railing and slowly rose, crossed over to her and picked up her hands. He brought one pair of their joined hands up, caught her chin with two of his fingers and lifted her face to his. Inches away, his gaze searched hers with an intensity she couldn't look away from.

"I care, Jenna. I care. Tell me what I have to do to prove it and I will." His breath warmed her cheek. His proximity should have caused her to freak out. That would have made sense. Toby's nearness was affecting her, but not in an unpleasant way. Far from it.

Wrestling her racing heartbeat, Jenna fought a desire to sag against him. To rest her head against his chest, cling to him and cry for all their lost years. But Toby didn't love her. Never would. He made that fact crystal clear years ago—his friendship with her was a dirty secret he didn't want anyone to know about. She wouldn't fall for that again. For him and his ability to say the right thing and act charming when it was just the two of them.

Besides, even if he were a changed man, she had changed, too. She wasn't his sweet, innocent, smiling friend anymore. No, she was damaged goods, ruined and closed off.

And she wanted to stay that way.

"I want things to be okay between us again," he whispered with a gentleness that tore at her heart.

Stay strong.

She'd allowed a man's kind words to fool her before. That's how Ross had gained her trust. Biggest mistake of her life. One she'd never make again.

"That's the problem, Toby. Don't you see? Some things will never be okay." She yanked her gaze from his, shoved out of his hold and rushed into the house. She didn't stop until she was upstairs in her room with the door closed. Jenna sank onto her bed, her entire body shaking. She dropped her head into her hands and focused on her breathing.

I care, Jenna. I care.

So much for discovering Toby's motives. Instead all she'd learned was that he was just as dangerous as before. And she was still a fool.

"That all looks just right. Thank you, son." Mr. Crest surveyed his new bedroom, his brow bunched in a mixture of acceptance and resignation. He folded his hands loosely in his lap.

Toby dragged the back of his arm over his forehead, clearing the sweat away.

After spending the morning working outside, Toby had moved indoors to clean out the office and move Mr. Crest's furniture downstairs. The man's motorized wheelchair had arrived earlier, and he was trying to be a good sport about it. When Toby's brother had finally been forced to rely on a chair, that had signaled the beginning of the end.

Toby's throat burned, making him swallow a couple times.

But Mr. Crest's situation was different. Very different. This wasn't Ben all over again, and it wasn't what had happened to Jenna's mom, either.

If Toby repeated those things thirty more times, would they sink in?

Mr. Crest motioned for Toby to follow him down the hallway, into the kitchen. "Jenna ran an idea past me this morning that I think merits your consideration."

"Oh?" Toby crossed to the sink and filled a glass with water. He chugged it, wiped his mouth with the back of his hand and filled it up again.

Jenna had avoided him all day. In fact, they hadn't spoken since their exchange on the back porch. Something had sparked between them as he held her hands and they shared a breath—something he had a hard time ignoring. Last night Toby had wanted to kiss Jenna. Badly.

Good thing she ran off.

A kiss would ruin everything. It was the reason he'd never made a move on her when they were teenagers, even though he'd had plenty of opportunities back then. Everything Toby touched broke. Every. Single. Thing. All except for his friendship with Jenna. That had been the only completely real and good thing in his life. With Jenna he'd laid himself bare—had been the real Toby— the one no one else seemed to want. She had never approached him with any expectations. She had simply accepted him as is and had chosen to be his friend.

Although, with how she was acting now, it looked like he had failed her after all.

Was he doomed to forever mess things up? His football dreams had ended with the knee injury. His romantic relationships never lasted longer than a month. The sporting-goods business he'd started in Florida had failed in its first year because his brick-and-mortar store couldn't compete with online prices. He'd had to look each of his employees in the eye and tell them their jobs were gone. The single mother who had managed the store for him had sobbed in his office; she hadn't known if she'd be able to feed her kids that month if the store closed.

He'd failed them all.

And his parents' faces when they'd bonded him out of jail for the drunk-driving arrests? Disappointed didn't even come close to describing them. It was something much heavier. More painful.

If Ben were alive, he wouldn't have shamed us like

this. He would have lived up to something. Done something worthwhile with his life. He wouldn't be a failure.

Now he could add knowing that he'd let down the people he cared about in Goose Harbor, too. Jenna wouldn't even look him in the eye most of the time.

No one was safe from his mistakes.

Toby set down his cup and jammed his hands into the pockets of his jeans. "So what was this idea?"

"There are three bedrooms upstairs. One, of course, we'll turn into the office—now that I'm down here. But that leaves an extra."

"The guest bedroom." Toby nodded.

Jenna's dad frowned, and a far-off look softened his weathered features. "Funny to hear it called that. Feels wrong. Our family always referred to that one as *Toby's room*." He shook his head slowly. "You were missed, for all these years. You were never forgotten here. I'm glad you're back with us."

"It's good to be back. I wish—" Toby swallowed hard. "I didn't realize how much I lost by staying away."

"You're talking about my daughter, aren't you?"

Toby scrubbed his hand down his face and let out a long breath. It wasn't worth hiding anything from Mr. Crest. The man possessed a gift for reading the truth on a person. "If only I could figure out how to fix things where she's concerned."

Mr. Crest clucked his tongue. "Me, too. I just don't know. These last few years—perhaps it's simply what happens when your child goes to college. She's my only one, so I have nothing to compare it to." He rubbed the knuckles on his left hand as if they ached. "But that place changed my girl. It stole something from her. I'm not certain if I'm making any sense."

Actually, he was making complete sense. And honestly, Toby wanted to cling to the idea Mr. Crest presented. Maybe Toby wasn't the reason behind her sadness and being closed off. Still, no matter the reason, Toby was determined to break through the wall she had up in order to win back his old best friend. He would release her from whatever cage she was locked in. To do that, though, he needed information—as much as he could get.

Toby hooked his hand on his shoulder, letting a muscle in his back burn with the stretch. "Did you notice a change in her right away, or was it more of a gradual thing?"

Mr. Crest narrowed his eyes and pursed his lips, deep in thought. "It was during her sophomore year. I'm not sure if you were aware, but she dropped out in the middle of that semester."

Alarms sounded in his head. The Jenna he knew loved learning. When they were teens, she used to excitedly tell him everything she'd discovered each day when they met on her back porch. Her eyes would light up and widen as her words tumbled out in such a rush that her sentences would end up jumbled together. Toby used to live for those nights, listening to her passionately share something new with him. Something that mattered to her. Something real.

Jenna choosing not to learn made his gut bunch. He'd known that she had taken six years to finish college but had assumed that the length was because she had loved taking classes and kept going. Not that she'd dropped out for a time. What had gone wrong?

"I didn't know that." Toby's voice sounded strained, even to his own ears. "Were her grades bad?"

"Nope." Mr. Crest looked tired. "Her grades were good up until that midpoint. Then one day she called out of the blue and told me she was on her way home and never wanted to go back. I tried to get her to talk." He shrugged. "She was hysterical. It scared me to hear her like that. To see her like that later. I couldn't even get her to go back to get the stuff out of her dorm room. I went on my own the next weekend and packed it up."

Sickness rocked through Toby. Something had happened to Jenna. Something terrible.

And he hadn't been there for her.

He took a shaky breath. "And she never said why?"

"I never pushed. She cried all the time back then… She's all I have. I worried that if I demanded an answer, I'd lose her. So instead I prayed a lot." He gripped the handrails on his wheelchair and shifted his position. "The next year she announced she was moving to Grand Rapids and wanted to start taking college courses online. But I don't believe she ever liked it there. From what I gather, she rarely left her apartment. The coffee shop she worked at was in the same building, and she never had to leave her place for the freelance writing she did."

"Has she dated anyone recently?" Toby's hand slipped on the counter. He had to move fast to catch himself from falling.

"No boyfriends." Her dad shook his head. "But I believe her heart's been taken for a very long time."

A very long time. Each word caused Toby's heart to crash into his ribs. He felt unsteady. He shoved his palm into his sternum and rubbed. She hadn't spent time with any guys besides him in high school. Was it someone from college? Had a guy broken her heart so badly that she'd run away?

He had to know. "By who?"

"That's not for me to tell. I probably said too much already." Jenna's dad leaned to adjust the part of his chair that cradled his calf muscles. "Anyway, we have a spare room, and the bunkhouse only has one bedroom. It might be nice to fix up your old room for Kasey. Give her a space that's all hers instead of having to share that tiny place with you." He held up a hand when Toby opened his mouth. "But *you* are her guardian. We don't want to step on your toes. Jenna and I both love Kasey, but we know our place. This is an option if you want it. That's all."

Toby sucked in a sharp breath. They loved Kasey, too? He wasn't alone in this. At least, not as alone as he felt. The four of them had found a way to form a tentative family unit, but the arrangement was still fragile. Any mistake on his part, any wrong move, risked costing Kasey everything. After all the child had been through, causing her any distress would be too high of a price. He had to work things out with Jenna. That was the only way he and Kasey could stay at the orchard without getting hurt.

Toby pressed away from the counter and swung his hands, clapping them in front of him. "Let's ask Kasey. I think she'll love the idea, as long as you and Jenna are sure that's all right. I don't want to impose any more than I already have. Kasey's my responsibility."

"Are you kidding? We'd love nothing more than for her to move in."

"I'll ask her, then. Today."

If Kasey did decide to move into the Crests' home, then that sealed it for how Toby would treat Jenna going forward. Kasey's happiness depended on him. If he acted on feelings of attraction or a tug of old camaraderie, he could ruin everything for Kasey. He wouldn't let her lose another home.

Chapter Seven

Jenna looped her arm over Kasey's tiny shoulders and steered her through the doorway into what would be her bedroom going forward. While Toby stayed back to tape and prep the walls, Jenna and Kasey had spent the morning shopping.

Toby had his back toward them when they entered the room. He wore faded jeans that fit like they had been made for him, a worn gray T-shirt and a blue-and-yellow baseball hat. He was barefoot, and for some reason that tugged at her, making Jenna soften toward him a little. The floorboard creaked under Jenna's foot, and Toby turned around at the noise. He shot her a boyish, excited grin. It was big enough to make the skin around his eyes crinkle.

Jenna froze, deeply aware of the fact that he was making her heart go berserk.

Why did he have to be so handsome? It wasn't fair.

Toby tapped the back wall of the old guest room. "Darker purple on this wall and lighter on the rest?"

Kasey groaned and turned toward Jenna. "He's hopeless, isn't he? Are all boys like that?"

Toby cocked his head. "Wait, what?"

Jenna hugged Kasey a little tighter for a minute. In the last few days, Kasey and Jenna had started bonding more. Everywhere they went, Kasey's soulful eyes followed Jenna. She was being watched, closely. What did the seven-year-old see? Jenna wanted to be someone Kasey could look up to, but Jenna needed to work on herself some before she could be a role model, starting with how she treated Toby. Teaching Kasey to hang on to bitterness and hurt wasn't healthy. Kasey shouldn't see her acting closed off, as if Jenna were some triple-locked door. Clinging to all that heartache wouldn't help her anymore—truthfully, it never had.

So why was Jenna *still* holding on to all of it?

She needed to let go of the past pain once and for all. For Kasey's sake, if not her own.

Being kind and having a functional relationship with Toby didn't mean that things had to go back to the way they were when they were kids. That would be impossible. *Never* would be far too soon to trust any man besides Dad. However, she could act cordially toward Toby without allowing him into her heart. From now on, she would treat Toby like she did other guys in town. It didn't need to be as difficult as she was making it.

Starting now.

She leaned close to Kasey's ear and stage-whispered, "Be patient with him. Colors are hard."

Toby's mouth dropped open in mock offense. "Ouch, ladies." He laid his hand over his heart and stumbled forward. "You wound me."

Kasey burst into a fit of giggles and launched toward him, grasping his hand. She tugged on him playfully.

"You're so silly. You don't know what the colors are? Good thing Jenna's here."

Toby's gaze captured Jenna's, and he winked before dropping down to Kasey's level. "Uh, I thought it was purple." He tapped the larger can of paint. "And…another lighterish purple." He pulled a comical face, playing up his confusion for Kasey, and looked up to Jenna for help. "I guess that's not right?"

Kasey hugged his neck, pressing her cheek against the side of his forehead. "Like I said. Hopeless."

But lovable. Jenna bit back the words that instantly begged to be added to Kasey's statement.

Watching them interact made warmth flood Jenna's chest. Toby was awesome with Kasey. If he ever decided to get married and add to his family, he would make an excellent father. When they were younger, Toby had often said he wasn't sure if he wanted children. He'd lived through losing Ben. Had seen firsthand how that tore at his parents. They'd stayed married and had loved Toby as best they could, but when Ben died, a part of them dimmed. They became emotionally and often physically detached from Toby, as if afraid that if they accidently loved him too much, he might get ripped away from them, too. Jenna knew her parents had tried to fill the gaps in her friend's life as best they could, but she was sure his parents' aloof attitude still affected him.

Toby grabbed at Kasey's middle, attacking her with tickles until she squealed with laughter. He planted a huge kiss on her cheek and secured the child snug in his arms, even though she tried to worm her way out, a smile taking over her small face. She was no match for that man's impressive muscles.

"Miss Crest, care to enlighten me? What colors are

we dealing with? Since this is clearly of utmost importance." His lips twitched.

Kasey stopped wiggling to look back and forth between them.

Jenna felt herself grinning back. "Well, sir, if you must know." She dropped to her knees nearby. "This is the color we'll use for the accent wall. It isn't simply purple."

"Oh, of course not." Toby braced his hands on the floor behind him and gave his head a solemn shake. It had been a long time since Jenna had joked with someone in such a carefree way. "Simply purple wouldn't do."

Jenna schooled her face as if this were the most serious topic ever. "*This* is February Berry."

"How did I not know that?" Toby rolled his eyes. He grabbed Kasey's little shoulders and gave a gentle shake. "I feel like such a fool."

Kasey pushed hair out of her eyes and looked over at Jenna. "See? What are we going to do with him? He's such a goof."

"I know," Jenna stage-whispered. "He's always been that way. And I fear there's no cure for him."

"Goof or not, my ears still work." Toby waggled his eyebrows.

Jenna's stomach fluttered. Were they flirting? They couldn't be… She was simply trying to be friendly again. That's all. Then again, she never teased Evan or Caleb this way, or her friend Jason, who ran the newspaper in town that she sometimes wrote freelance articles for.

She dropped her gaze away from Toby's and tapped the second paint can. "The lighter one here, we'll use it on the remaining three walls. It's a really pretty color called A Winter's Kiss."

"A kiss, huh?" Toby got to his feet and ruffled Kasey's hair before she scampered away. He leaned closer and squinted at the paint in question. "I didn't know a kiss could be a color. Did you?" he asked Jenna.

It felt like the air had been suctioned out of the room. "No. I, ah…" Her voice was so small. "I don't know anything about kisses like that."

Over Kasey's head, he caught Jenna's gaze again and kept it. Something she couldn't quite identify pulsed between. Sympathy? Understanding?

Toby's smile was soft, with a hint of sadness. "All right, we've got some painting to get done, then. Let's get to it." He pointed at Kasey. "You probably don't want to work in those clothes. They're way too nice."

The little girl had insisted on getting decked out in a dress and flowered headband for her girls' time with Jenna.

Kasey stuck out her bottom lip in an exaggerated way. "I don't have anything to wear."

Jenna grabbed a screwdriver and pried the lid off A Winter's Kiss. "I have shirts you can toss on over what you're wearing." She pointed the screwdriver in the direction of her bedroom. "Go into my room and open the second drawer of my dresser that's closest to the door. Grab whatever you want and toss it on. They're all old work shirts."

"Thanks, Jenna!" Kasey zigzagged around her and pounded into the hallway.

Toby reached for the screwdriver and eased it out of her hand. His eyebrows rose. "You okay?"

"Oh, yeah, sure." Jenna located the stirring stick and

dipped it into the lighter paint. "I meant to tell you, you're doing a great job with her. I really respect what you've done—accepting the responsibility of a guardian is not an easy thing."

He kneaded his temple with his hand. "The option in the will was for me to be her guardian or for her to go to foster care. I couldn't do that to her."

"Like I said, I really respect that—respect you."

"That means a lot." He sounded hoarse. He cleared his throat and then bent over to straighten a drop cloth. "Thanks for spending time with her today. I can tell she really looks up to you."

Jenna got up and brushed off the back of her jeans, just for something to do. "She's a great kid."

"My cousin wasn't the best mom. The night that…" He looked away. Jenna traced the line of his strong profile with her eyes. His Adam's apple bobbed. "She left Kasey on her own a lot. Sophia was still into partying." He shook his head, as if the words hurt coming out. "That night she left Kase all alone. She drank too much—way too much. They think she just fell into the lake off the walkway and was too toasted to even try to swim."

"I'm so sorry." Jenna laid her hand on his forearm. Holding back in that moment would have felt wrong. Friends comforted each other. That's all the gesture meant. "I know you always cared about Sophia."

"She was the only cousin I had on either side of the family." He pushed at the drop cloth with his toe. "But I'm disappointed in how she treated her daughter. Kasey saw a lot of neglect at her hands. It sounds like the fridge was often bare."

Jenna added pressure to where her hand rested on

his arm to make him look at her. "Kasey never has to face that again. Not with you. You'll always take care of her. I think she already looks at you like a father. She really loves you."

"She's attached herself to you, too. Back at the bunkhouse, she talks about you all the time." He scrubbed his hand over his jaw. "You know, I'll miss her not being there with me." He picked up Jenna's hand and cupped it between both of his. "I'm doing the right thing for her though, right?"

She worked her bottom lip between her teeth. "Tobe," she breathed. "You know you're welcome in the house whenever you want. Your family is here."

"Is it?"

His thumb skated in a gentle circle over the back of her hand. The tenderness in his eyes flashed heat through her veins. Despite the bad blood between them, if he leaned in right now, she'd let him kiss her. Correction: if he got too much closer, she was liable to bunch her free hand into his shirt and yank him toward her. Toby Holcomb was dangerous that way; he always had been. He—his presence alone—did something to her.

Kasey chose that moment to tromp back into the room. She held up a blue jersey with Holcomb printed on the back. "Look, Toby. Jenna has a whole drawer of your stuff."

Jenna let out a squeak and scuttled away from Toby as if his touch suddenly burned her. She snatched the shirt out of Kasey's hands, but the girl's startled expression shot guilt into Jenna movements, making her slow down. Surely Kasey hadn't intended to embarrass her, but opening that drawer, letting Toby *know* a drawer like that even existed, was akin to taking a crowbar to Jenna's heart and peeling it open to reveal her most guarded secret. She still loved Toby. Always had. Always would. No matter what.

Talk about hopeless.

"Not that one, sweetie." Jenna clutched the shirt to her chest. She peeked over at Toby, and her throat spasmed. If his wide eyes were any indication, he recognized his old high school jersey.

Jenna bounced her gaze away. "That's the…it's the wrong drawer. I'll get you something else." She pivoted to leave and stumbled over their painting supplies, tipping forward. Moving faster than she would have believed possible, Toby was at her side, his hands on her upper arms, making sure she didn't fall down.

"Careful there." He hung on to her arm until she allowed her gaze to collide with his. Her stomach did a flip-flop as he searched her face, his mouth open, incredulous. "You still have all that stuff? The things I gave you?"

Jenna brushed his hand away. "I'll be back in a second."

He let her go, but she felt his eyes on her as she left. Seconds later in her bedroom, Jenna closed the door, pressed her back into it and slid to the floor. She pushed her forehead into Toby's old shirt and focused on making her breaths even. Once she felt more in control of her emotions, she pulled herself back to her feet and crossed over to the second dresser in her room. She couldn't be upset with Kasey. The girl hadn't been trying to humiliate her. Logically, depending on how she had judged the distance, either of Jenna's two dressers could be described as closest to the door. Jenna should have just fetched a shirt herself.

She tugged open her Toby drawer, refolded the shirt, traced her fingers over the name and finally placed it back inside. The drawer held gifts he'd given her—letters, pictures and a few of his old shirts that he'd lent or given her at one time or another when they were teens. A smart woman would have parted with all these things a long time ago.

She slid the drawer closed.

Apparently, Jenna wasn't very smart.

Toby paced the hallway.

Dishes clanked in the sink, and sweet notes of cinnamon hung in the air from the apple dumplings and vanilla-bean ice cream they'd wolfed down a few minutes ago. Jenna was in the kitchen clearing up dinner, and Mr. Crest and Kasey were locking horns in a game of checkers in the front room. A tiny cry of "King me!" let him know Kasey was doing just fine in there.

The floor groaned beneath his feet.

Jenna had shooed them all out after dinner, insisting she didn't need help.

But *he* needed help.

Jenna's laughed wrapped its way around his heart and squeezed. "Are you going to come in here, or are you pretty satisfied to wear a hole through those floorboards?"

Busted.

Toby swung around the edge of the doorway, into the kitchen.

"Every piece of this old house creaks." Jenna leaned against the counter near the wide sink, arms crossed, hair up in a high ponytail and a dish towel tossed over her shoulder. Stunning.

His mouth went dry, and for a moment, he couldn't have spoken even if his life depended on it. Before him stood a woman who was kindhearted and encouraging, who welcomed an orphaned child into her heart without any questions, cared for her father with unmatched devotion and gave up her career pursuits to return home. When the situation called for it, she lasted ten hours on her feet doing manual labor in the orchards without uttering a single complaint. She could scrape paint and fix steps with more gusto than he could and later whip up a meal that tasted better than any restaurant he'd ever been to.

For the first time in a long time, Toby felt like he was home.

Being around Jenna gave him hope again. Toby wanted to be the person she had long ago believed in. Jenna was the only person who ever saw beyond his football-player facade and popular-guy swagger to get to know and appreciate him as he was instead of who he felt like he had to pretend to be.

She arched her eyebrow. "Are you going to tell me what you're thinking? Because you've been standing there for—" she played like she was looking at a watch on her wrist "—a good two minutes and still haven't explained the reason behind all that pacing."

Oh, right. He'd been staring longer than was polite.

He worked at a nagging muscle in his neck. "Kasey came home with a note from her teacher."

She crossed to the table and sat down, patting the spot at the head of the table. "Continue."

He tugged the slip of paper from his pocket and laid it on the table so Jenna could read the short note. Then he dropped down into the chair.

Jenna rolled her shoulders once. "I still don't get what your question is. This has a number and says 'Call me.'"

Toby dropped his hands, palms up, onto the table. "What does it mean?"

Jenna's lips quirked, and she drummed her fingers on the tabletop. "One would assume she wants you to call her."

"Great." He sent her a smirk. "From now on you should go by Sherlock."

Her eyebrows shot up. "Excuse me, bucko, but you're the one who came to me for advice."

He could toss back another flirtatious comment or he could say what was on his heart. Toby had spent a lifetime faking his way through conversations, through relationships. But being back at the orchard had given him a sort of mental rewind button, allowing him to re-think the last ten years of his life. For once, he wanted to be himself—completely and totally himself—and say the truthful thing that came to mind.

"Well, that's because your opinion is the only one that ever really mattered to me."

Jenna's smile dropped. She laced her fingers together and studied them. "Did Kasey know anything about it— about what Leah wants to tell you?"

So much for being real. His mood nose-dived.

If she was going to act like he hadn't said that, so would he. "See, that's the weirdest part. Kasey said she's still a little shy at school but she hasn't gotten into trouble or had any problems with anyone."

But was Kasey struggling and he hadn't noticed? Toby should have known he'd crash and burn at being a guardian. Everything he touched crumbled. Why had he expected anything else?

Jenna's posture relaxed. "Okay, but last weekend, didn't you ask Leah to keep you updated and to let you know if she noticed anything about Kasey? She's probably honoring that. Maybe she spotted something about Kasey and she wants to make you aware of it. If so, that's good. Call her."

Self-doubt rattled against his rib cage. "Here's the thing—what if I don't know how to deal with whatever she has to tell me? Sometimes I wonder if it's better to not know something. Then you don't have to deal with it." Although, could he convince himself that was true anymore? No. Even if he ignored a problem, in the end, that *was* dealing with it. Just badly. Besides, managing his life that way hadn't gone well.

Jenna rubbed her thumb over a pattern in the wood grain. "Why would you want to fake your way through something so important?"

"I... I've been faking my way through my entire life." That burned coming out. He swallowed hard. "You know that."

"Toby." The way she said his name, so soft and sad, seemed to hold every emotion under the sun, from frustration to pity.

He shrugged. "I don't know what I'm doing when it comes to Kasey. What if I mess everything up?"

She dropped her chin into her hand. "I mean, do any of us ever actually know what we're doing, about anything? Honestly, I would guess that a lot of parenting is praying your way through situations you don't have a clue how to handle."

"Pray your way through situations you don't have a clue about." He shook his head and wagged his finger.

"You know, I think that's going to be my life motto from now on."

"It would do me well to adopt it, too." She blew out a long stream of air, stirring wisps of hair that had worked their way out of her messy ponytail.

It took every ounce of his self-discipline not to reach over and cup the side of her face. Skim his fingers over to the soft skin he was sure to find in the place where her jaw met her neck. Lean across the distance and taste the lingering sweetness from dessert on her lips.

He was a mess. Three days of Jenna talking to him, joking with him, and he was a goner. Where had his resolve to act businesslike with her gone? The feelings coursing through him would only muddle up everything he was working toward. Kasey loved the Crests, loved her new bedroom and loved living on the orchard. Acting on emotion could cost them their home, his livelihood. It was too steep a price, especially when he still didn't know why Jenna had been angry with him or what had happened to her in college.

Toby fisted his hands and tucked them under the table.

She straightened her spine and crossed her legs. "I'm going to sit here until you make that call." She pretended to examine her nails. "I've got all night."

Her mannerisms tricked a breathy laugh out of him. He fished his phone from his pocket and punched in the number. It rang twice.

A female voice answered, "Hello?"

"Hi. This is Toby Holcomb. I'm looking for Miss Vincent, Kasey's teacher."

"I'm so glad you called. Please, call me Leah from now on, all right?"

He peeked over at Jenna. She moved her hand in a "get on with it" motion.

"Did you want to tell me something about Kasey?"

"All things considered, Kasey is doing excellent. The counseling group I suggested for her seems to be helping her cope."

He might as well ask about the one thing he'd been wondering about. "She keeps talking about a boy named Alex. It sounds like he's in that after-school group, too. Do you know who that is?" Kasey was only seven, but Toby knew how important childhood friends were and the sort of impact the right—and wrong—people could have on a young person's life.

"That's probably Alex Atwood. He's adopted and only recently came to town. He's a year younger than Kasey."

He knew the name Atwood. The patriarch of the Atwood family, Sesser, was a business tycoon who made his wealth from real estate he owned, sold and rented throughout a vast region spanning the lower-west region of Michigan, wrapping around the lake, reaching all the way to Chicago, where he had large holdings. Sesser had one daughter, Claire, a pretty redhead who was a few years older than Toby. Alex must be Claire's son. That solved, it was time to steer the conversation back to discovering why Kasey's teacher had requested he call in the first place.

"Miss Vincent?"

"Leah."

"Right." He ran his fingers through his hair and tugged. "So Kasey is doing well?"

"Toby, I didn't have you call to talk about Kasey."

"You didn't?"

"I wanted to ask you out on a date, actually. Kasey told me you're not married."

"I'm flattered, but I'm…" His eyes went right to Jenna's. He took a rattling breath. "I'm taken."

Miss Vincent groaned lightly. "Well, that's crummy, but I'm glad I asked. You never know unless you ask, and all that. I hope this doesn't bring about any awkwardness between us. I just figured, well…you're *Toby Holcomb*. In the flesh, you know? I had such a crush on you in high school and watched all your college games so I could fangirl over you."

Had they known each other? Was he that oblivious that he didn't remember? "We went to school together?"

"I'm three years younger. I don't think we'd ever spoken to each other until last Sunday. But I always had a thing for you."

Except she didn't have a thing for him. Only for the fraud who had walked the hallways of Goose Harbor High School. Whatever her idea of Toby Holcomb was, it wasn't him.

After another minute of pleasantries, they hung up.

Jenna cocked her head. "I only heard one end of that conversation, but did she just ask you out?"

He nodded.

"Leah's very nice." Jenna laced her fingers together and placed them in her lap. "Can I ask why you told her you were taken?"

"Because I am." He shrugged. "Like you and I were saying the other night, my family is here. You understand that, don't you?"

"Of course—that makes sense." She braced her hands on the table and nodded. "You're taken by your commitment to Kasey."

"Right. Kasey." He snagged Jenna's hand. "Besides, I'm not interested in dating anyone."

"You don't want to date?" Her voice faltered. "Not at all?"

He shook his head slowly. "It's not even on my radar. I don't think I'll ever date anyone." Did she understand what he was really saying? *I'll be here. I'll stay with you. After your dad... I want to be your best friend again, forever.*

"Do you want to... It's late, but do you want to...?" She glanced over her shoulder to the door that led outside.

Toby squeezed her hand once and let it go. "I'd love to sit on the back porch with you tonight."

And every night after that.

FREE Merchandise and a Cash Reward[†] are 'in the Cards' for you!

Dear Reader,

We're giving away FREE MERCHANDISE and a CASH REWARD!

Seriously, we'd like to reward you for reading this novel by giving you **FREE MERCHANDISE** worth over $20 retail plus a CASH REWARD! And no purchase is necessary!

You see the Jack of Hearts sticker above? Paste that sticker in the box on the Free Merchandise Voucher inside. Return the Voucher today... and we'll send you Free Merchandise plus a Cash Reward!

Thanks again for reading one of our novels—and enjoy your Free Merchandise and Cash Reward with our compliments!

Pam Powers

Pam Powers

P.S. Look inside to see what Free Merchandise is **"in the cards"** for you!

W

e'd like to send you two free books like the one you are enjoying now. Your two books have a combined price of over $10 retail, but they are yours to keep absolutely FREE! We'll even send you 2 wonderful surprise gifts and a Cash Reward†. You can't lose!

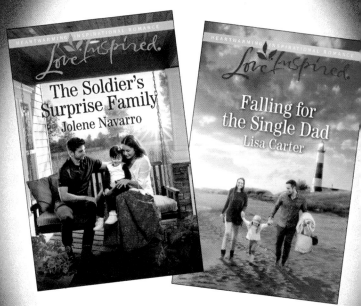

REMEMBER: Your Free Merchandise, consisting of **2 Free Books** and **2 Free Gifts**, is worth over $20 retail! Plus we'll send you a **Cash Reward** (it's a dollar) which is really the icing on the cake because it's in addition to your FREE Merchandise! No purchase is necessary, so please send for your Free Merchandise today.

Get TWO FREE GIFTS!

We'll also send you 2 wonderful FREE GIFTS (worth about $10 retail), in addition to your 2 Free books and Cash Reward!

Visit us at:
www.ReaderService.com

Books received may not be as shown.

YOUR FREE MERCHANDISE INCLUDES...
2 FREE Books **AND** 2 FREE Mystery Gifts
PLUS you'll get a Cash Reward†

FREE MERCHANDISE VOUCHER

2 FREE
BOOKS
and
2 FREE
GIFTS

Please send my Free Merchandise, consisting of
2 Free Books and **2 Free Mystery Gifts** PLUS my
Cash Reward. I understand that I am under no
obligation to buy anything, as explained
on the back of this card.

❑ I prefer the regular-print edition
105/305 IDL GLJQ

❑ I prefer the larger-print edition
122/322 IDL GLJQ

Please Print

FIRST NAME

LAST NAME

ADDRESS

APT.#   CITY

STATE/PROV.   ZIP/POSTAL CODE

NO PURCHASE NECESSARY!

LI-N16-FMC15

▲ Detach card and mail today. No stamp needed. ▲

® and ™ are trademarks owned by the publisher and/or its licensee. Printed in the U.S.A.

READER SERVICE—Here's how it works:

BUSINESS REPLY MAIL

FIRST-CLASS MAIL PERMIT NO. 717 BUFFALO, NY

POSTAGE WILL BE PAID BY ADDRESSEE

READER SERVICE
PO BOX 1867
BUFFALO NY 14240-9952

NO POSTAGE
NECESSARY
IF MAILED
IN THE
UNITED STATES

Chapter Eight

Streams of sunlight blotted across the floor of the Crest Country Store. Jenna trailed her fingers over the antique wooden countertop. Along with many of the shelving areas of the store, it had been constructed out of re-claimed siding from the original barn located on the Crest property when her great-grandfather purchased the plot. She pressed her palms flat against it, feeling all the worn grooves. Her history.

Her future, too.

Each day it became easier to give up on the dream she'd worked toward with all the online courses she'd taken to earn her degree. Tucked away on the far edge of Goose Harbor, she'd never become an award-winning journalist. It had been a silly goal all along, really. Her disposition wasn't suited for chasing stories or wiggling information out of people. No one would describe her as a go-getter. Yet it splintered her heart to let go of writing all the same.

She released a loud puff of air and pressed her palm to her forehead.

So basically God wanted her to give up anything

she'd ever wanted out of her life. Her desire to be a mother, to marry a good man, to have many years with her father—instead she'd witness piece after excruciating piece of him float away—any independence or safety she imagined she had and her hope of one day publishing something that mattered. As if she were an apple being ground in the press until all the cider was crushed out of her, she felt like she had nothing left to cling to...just pulp.

How was that for God's supposed fair and impartial treatment?

She straightened a couple items in the baked-goods area, her boots clipping across the floor. "If You don't want me to have any of those things—" she stocked the pie area with a little more force than required "—what *do* You want with me?"

The automated door on the side of the store attached to the accessibility ramp whined as it opened. Dad entered in his wheelchair, smiling like Christmas morning. "Can you believe this place?" He whistled long and low, clearly impressed. "What you and Toby have done with the whole orchard... I should have handed it over to the both of you years ago."

Dad spoke as if she and Toby were one entity. While Jenna and Toby had worked out a comfortable peace over the past two weeks, they were hardly together. Although, after she'd overheard him turn down Leah, the two of them had started to spend more time together— going on strolls through the orchard, checking the trees together, taking Kasey to watch him coach the team at football practice. Evenings were spent on the porch swing, sipping hot cider and discussing the game plan for the next day.

Hearing that Toby had zero interest in anything romantic had allowed Jenna to put her guard down. A tiny part of her was beginning to believe that they might be able to revive a semblance of their old friendship.

Maybe Dad meant "both of you" as though they were a team. A "Go Crest Orchard staff!" kind of meaning.

However, she had to dispel any thoughts he was clinging to about making mistakes with how he'd managed the orchard. Believing something like that would hurt him.

"Except Toby wouldn't have been here, and as much as I wanted to believe I could, I couldn't handle everything on my own. Not with the same results, at least. Most of this, okay, all of this, is thanks to Toby." She unlocked the front entry and flipped the sign to Open. "But don't kick yourself about the timing—remember, he's only here for Kasey, so *years ago* he wouldn't have been available to help us."

Dad leaned on the armrest. "If you truly believe he's only here for Kasey, then you're not as quick as I've always given you credit for."

"Dad, please," she whispered.

He fisted his hand where it rested and sat up a little straighter. "Honeybee, I think I've done you a disservice. After we lost your mom, I was afraid to lose you, too. In any sense of the word. Because of that, I never pushed or challenged you. I rarely questioned your choices. I let you hide—from me, from yourself—because I rationalized that helping you avoid discomfort was a way to show love. Which was wrong. I failed you in that way."

Her stomach bunched into a giant knot that threatened to climb into her throat. He had no idea what he was talking about. "Trust me when I say I had plenty of my share of discomfort with or without your protection."

Fact was, she cherished how he sheltered her. She needed it. Didn't she? On the flip side, he had enabled her to live as a hermit for the past seven years. He'd paid for her apartment in Grand Rapids while she was still studying. If he hadn't done that, she would have drowned in all her fear and anxiety. Then again, perhaps she would have been forced to face it all head-on.

Drown or fight? Yeah, she'd done neither. Jenna had existed like a mole. Underground. Eyes closed.

She wasn't half as independent as she'd tricked herself into believing.

He moved his chair closer and dropped his voice. "I assume that you've seen bad times on your own, but my failure came from never walking you through the challenging things. Now the second you feel insecure, you turn inward. You block out everyone to protect yourself."

And that was a problem because…?

Jenna tried to swallow a couple of times, but the lump in her throat was far too large. Instead of trying to speak, she crossed her arms and raised her eyebrows.

"That's a sad and scary way to live, darling," Dad said.

Great. Even he thought her life was pathetic.

"Don't hold back, Daddy."

He slowly shook his head, his eyes closed, as if the conversation pained him. "Any longer, I don't intend to. I won't, because I love you, and love—true love— does the hard things. God doesn't want you living like this either. He has better things planned for you, if only you'd believe that."

"Better? Ha. Like what?" Jenna tossed up her hands.

"Besides, what's so bad about being here and taking care of this orchard for the rest of my life? Maybe that's what I'm meant to do."

"Running this place can be a very God-honoring mission. Anything can be if your heart is following God. At least, I like to think so. I hope that I've lived my life in a way that showed His love every day."

"You always have, Dad," she said, her voice soft. "Every day. I've always admired that about you. You've shown love to every person who walked onto our property. You had a huge ministry by letting widows and young, struggling moms live in the bunkhouse over the years. You…you've always been so good." Her voice broke. "It's one of the reasons I don't understand why you don't struggle more with your diagnosis. You don't deserve to suffer."

He closed his eyes, pinched the bridge of his nose and took in a breath that made his shoulders rise. "Listen. I can choose to dwell on the bad, but where would that get me? My illness is progressive—this is only going to get worse. So I can ruin today, when it might be the best day healthwise I'm going to have for the rest of my life, or I can cherish it. I'm trying to do the latter—not always successfully, mind you, but that's my focus. I choose to soak in the sights of you and Toby and Kasey, my home, my Bible and my orchard because I might lose the ability to see all that tomorrow." He shifted in his seat. "I refuse to live with the regret of what I didn't do today."

Her chest tightened. Had Dad been having trouble with his eyes? Now wasn't the time to ask, not in the midst of this conversation, but she tucked that away to question him about later. "If only I'd been blessed with half as much strength as you."

"Strength isn't a character trait. It's a choice. Strength happens in the moments when you don't think you possess the ability to go on but you keep going anyway. Speaking of which." He jutted his thumb to indicate the direction of the orchard. "It's high time for you to confront whatever happened between you and Toby."

Jenna forced out a laugh and turned away, in search of the apron she wore while working in the shop. "That's so far in the past it doesn't even matter anymore."

"If it doesn't matter, then why are you allowing it to stop you from loving that man?"

She hooked her fingers on the edge of the counter, afraid to let go. "Dad, I don't—"

"Come on, now. Give your old man some credit." His voice was gentle but persistent. "You've been in love with that man since he was a boy. You love him so much it terrifies you. The question is, are you my brave little Jenna—the one who used to shimmy up the tallest trees in the orchard, sit on the highest branch and throw her head back, arms out toward the sunshine? Or are you the Jenna who's spent the last six months creeping around this house, petrified of her own shadow?"

She stalked around the countertop and turned on the computer they used as a register. "A person is liable to get hurt perched out on the highest limb."

"True. But they'll also soak in the best sunshine."

"Dad, can we just stop with the—"

"I never said it was without risk. Everything is risk. Don't you see that? If you put your heart out there, you risk being rejected. If you keep your heart to yourself, you risk being overlooked, missing out, never knowing love. Risk is always present, honeybee. Especially when we think we're protecting ourselves, because that means risking friendship, memories and love. So who are you really protecting? Because living like *that* doesn't sound to me like taking good care of your heart or the life God's given you."

The tiny buzzer over the doorway sounded, interrupting their conversation. Jenna leaned around a flower display to see and recognized Jason Moss's moppy brown hair right away. Jason was a Goose Harbor lifer, but more important, he was the editor of the town's only newspaper. In his untucked button-down and khakis, he always looked the part of small-town reporter.

"You win the grand prize." She moved around the table and brushed past Dad to greet him. "The first person to the store this season."

Jason latched on to the strap of his ever-present messenger bag. "Wow. Is that so? And what do I win?"

"My esteem."

He laughed. "That'll do." He glanced around the store. "I'm meeting up with my cousin and her son after this, so I'm going to take some of your famous cider donuts and at least one of these pies." He picked up an apple pie drenched in caramel sauce. "But I also have a proposition for you."

Jenna gathered his things and made for the register. "A proposition? This sounds intriguing."

Dad cleared his throat. "I'm heading out to the orchard to see how Toby and the crew are doing."

"Okay, see you later." She waved and then turned her attention back to Jason.

"Want me to give Toby any messages from you?"

Oh, Dad was a rat.

He must have thought Jason was about to make a move on her, and this was Dad's way of saying which man got his vote. Little did he know that over the past few months, Jenna had submitted writing samples to Jason. As an editor, he was a man with a lot of connections in the newspaper business. She'd figured it was worth a try.

"Sure." Jenna rang up Jason's items. "Tell the *whole crew* to be safe out there today. No crazy climbing to the highest limbs."

Dad harrumphed but finally left the store.

With her hands on her hips, Jenna surveyed the store. Only four hours into opening day, and the shelves already looked like a scene out of a dystopian movie—bare. She'd misjudged their popularity. Then again, she hadn't been aware until Jason stopped by that he was going to run a front-page article about the orchard in today's paper. Free marketing.

The handful of ladies who helped bake and run the shop every season hadn't been able to work during opening weekend because of an event going on downtown. The Crests' little store was open only Saturdays and for a few hours on Sundays, and the first days of the season were usually slow. But after the business she'd juggled today, it looked like it would be a very late night working in the kitchen to ensure that they'd have enough stock for tomorrow. It was all right though—during orchard season the Crests had always taken Monday as their day off. As much as she disliked working on Sundays, many people—police officers, nurses, pilots, gas attendants, pastors—had to work on the typical day of rest in order for the world to function.

With the lack of goods left, perhaps they should close early.

The buzzer sounded, and a gasping Kasey burst through the door. "Quick! Toby's hurt! You have to come. He needs you." She latched on to Jenna's arm, dissolving into tears.

A tingle of nausea rocked through Jenna's body while shivers raced over her skin.

What happened? How bad is he hurt?

But she wouldn't waste time on questions. She needed to take action and make a choice now to be strong. She focused on her breathing while she locked each door and flipped the sign to Closed. She extended her hand to Kasey. "Take me to him."

The little girl's body was trembling worse than Jenna's. "He fell from a ladder. Your dad told him not to use that one, but the other guys were using the apple ladders, and you know Toby."

"I do. He's pretty stubborn." Jenna leaned down and folded the little girl into a hug.

Toby knew better than to use any old ladder for harvesting apples. Root systems guaranteed that nothing in an orchard was flat. Normal household ladders were prone to tipping over on the unstable ground. They trained all the hands on their first day on the importance of using only the orchard ladders with adjustable legs that allowed for a stable platform no matter what angle they were set at.

But that knowledge wouldn't help a scared little girl. "We'll make sure he's okay."

"What if he dies?" The girl sobbed, her words breaking. "What would happen to me? Would I be homeless?"

Jenna pulled Kasey into another fierce hug. "This is your home. Always. No matter what. Understand?" She ran her hand down her long hair. "And Toby will be fine. My dad would have called an ambulance if he was seriously injured."

"You'll take care of him?" Kasey clung to Jenna's waist.

"I will. I promise."

Dad was waiting outside. He snagged Kasey before they made it into the house. "He's resting on the couch in the front room. Kasey and I will open the store back up." He motioned Jenna to lean in so he could whisper. "I don't want her going back in there until she calms down."

Jenna agreed and went in alone. Dad hadn't mentioned if Toby was bleeding or whether he would require medical attention, probably due to Kasey's presence.

She found Toby on the edge of the couch, ramrod straight with his arms crossed, wearing a full pout. "I'm fine. Whatever they said, don't believe it. I'm fine." He looked like an angry little boy who'd been told he had to sit out during kickball. It was ridiculously adorable.

She attempted to school her face but felt the tick of her lips trying to grin. "So did you or did you not fall off a ladder?"

He relaxed his arms and grumbled, "Well, that part's true."

She crossed to the couch and stopped right in front of him, scanning him for bumps and bruises. No blood. That was a good sign. "Where did you land?"

"On the ground." Now he fought a smile.

"Oh, you're hilarious. Let's sign you up for the circus." She laughed. "You know, I *could* just go get Dad and Kasey and have them freak out all over again." She pivoted, as if she was about to leave.

"Please, seriously, anything but that." He grabbed

her wrist. "They were treating me like I wasn't going to make it." He tugged her back toward him. "I may or may not have landed on my shoulders. And possibly my head."

"Toby!" She dropped a knee onto the couch beside him and her fingers flew into his hair, working over his head, feeling for the—yup, there it was—huge bump.

"Ouch." Toby shrank away from her probing hand. "Don't press on that part, but if you want to keep running your fingers through my hair, I won't stop you."

She laid her hand on his shoulder and used him for balance as she stood. "You're impossible."

"You love it." He winked.

His goofy grin caused her heart to somersault away from her and land somewhere near him. Then again, Dad was right. Her heart had always belonged to Toby.

But he never needed to learn that. She wouldn't be that foolish girl again, forever waiting for him to notice her. No matter what Dad said, romance was a closed book in her life. It was better that way.

Jenna fetched an ice pack from the freezer and then pressed it against the lump on his head. "Lean back so I can wedge this between you and the back of the couch." She got Toby situated and then stayed beside him, angling her body so she could watch him. Everything was catching up as her adrenaline rush faded. Toby seemed like he was okay, but this could have been a very different scenario. What if he'd been badly hurt? Tightness crept across her chest.

His gaze moved over her face, too, tracing from her eyes to her lips and back again. "Jenna, I'm okay. It's nothing."

She nodded and let out a shaky breath. "You could

have been really hurt though. I don't want anything to happen to you."

A soft smile highlighted the handsome planes of his face. "I shouldn't like hearing that as much as I do."

Dad's words about living each day without regrets came back to her. Fear had stolen so many years from her. Was it possible to be that girl soaking in the sunshine again? Sitting at the treetop, arms stretched out at her sides and her head tipped toward the clouds. An image of total trust. It struck her that her spiritual posture should be the same as that, too. Reaching out in faith, climbing any obstacle in her life so she could get as close to Jesus as possible. Knowing that she could get hurt—being exposed and open—but trusting and having faith anyway. *Living.*

It could all start by forgiving Toby.

She clasped her hands in her lap. "I want you to know that I'm not mad at you anymore."

He frowned. "I've been thinking about that a lot, actually. Was it because I wasn't there for you when your mom died?"

She nodded. "That was the start. You didn't even stay by me at the funeral."

He sat up a little and grabbed the ice pack from behind him to prevent it from sliding down his back. "I know it's not an excuse, but I loved her a lot, and losing her really bowled me over. I didn't know how to be there for you, like you were there for me with Ben." He focused all his attention on the ice pack in his hands. "I was upset and angry and thought that wouldn't help you."

Men. Were they all so dense? "I *needed* you. Your

presence. Just you breathing beside me. How did you not see that? You were my best friend."

He squeezed the ice pack, making it melt quicker. "I couldn't have said anything to make it better though. I thought me talking would make it worse."

Jenna rested her hand on his arm. "I didn't need you to say or fix anything." She dropped her voice. "I just wanted you there. I wanted you beside me, holding my hand."

He leaned his head back against the couch. "I'm so sorry. If I could change how I acted, I would."

"But it's not just that. When I had to start going to the high school, I was so excited because although I was afraid, my best friend would be there. But you ignored me. You'd walk past me in the hallway without even making eye contact. After spending time together almost every day for our entire lives, you pretended you didn't know me." Her voice shook. "Do you know how much that hurt?"

"I feel really bad about that." He let the ice pack drop to the ground, and he eased forward. "I thought the other students, especially the guys I hung with, would make fun of you more if they knew how much I cared about you. I thought I was protecting you."

"Again." She tapped his arm. "I didn't need you to protect me. I just wanted you there. With me."

He placed his elbows on his knees and dropped his head into his hands. "I was such a jerk. There's no explanation for it. I was a selfish, stupid teenage boy who wanted everyone to like me."

Emboldened by the last few days they'd spent together and the sincerity lacing his words, Jenna tucked her hand under his chin and drew his face out of his hands so she could capture his gaze. "Except they didn't actually know you, Toby. They liked that guy you pretended to be at school."

"I know." His fingers inched up her arm and took the hand away from his chin. He cradled it in both of his. "My whole life has been a huge parade with so many different masks. Every part of my life...except when I'm with you. You're the only person who ever saw me, Jenna. I... I..."

Whatever he was trying to say, Jenna wasn't sure if she was prepared for it.

She pressed her hand into his. "You didn't just ignore me. I heard you making fun of the orchard and my dad when people asked you about it. And you called me Amish Lady!"

"That was a joke between us. I used to call you that when we were really young." His brow scrunched. "That never bothered you before then."

"But everyone at school *heard* you. People threw those white head caps at me in the hallway for the next two years. Someone broke into my locker and filled it with friendship-bread dough—it ruined all my books." None of the things she was listing seemed like a big deal now, but to a shy sixteen-year-old girl who suddenly felt like she didn't have a friend in the world, the teasing had shattered her. "On my birthday they left a pile of boxes at my locker full of those faceless rag dolls, and I never stopped getting teased about it. 'Will your dad show up with a buggy, Jenna? Must have been cold last winter without electricity.'"

"I didn't know it was ever that bad. You being angry with me makes total sense now. *I'm* angry with me." He let go of her hand and pressed his fingers across his forehead so his eyes were shielded. "I failed you in every sense of the word."

She kept her hand on his thigh, needing the connection while talking about the past. "It was as if you were ashamed of me. I think that's what broke me the most."

"Never." He dropped his hand and scooted closer so there was no space between them. "I was never ashamed of you. I was ashamed of myself." His eyes blazed with an intensity that warmed her. "That boy who did those things to you? I hated him—then and now. But believe me, I'm not him anymore. I would never do those—"

She put her fingers over his mouth. "I know," she whispered. "I… I trust you, Toby. I've seen the changes in your life. You're hardworking and obviously devoted to the orchard. It's clear you look up to my dad. You care."

He lightly removed her hand from his face and then flipped it palm up. "I care." He placed a kiss on the exact spot where her wrist met her hand, and then he whispered, "More than you know."

Warmth from his words feathered against her soft skin, raising goose bumps on her arms. Her heart felt like it was going to pound through her shirt.

"I forgive you." Wow, her voice was embarrassingly breathy, but she couldn't control it. Toby's kiss had been the most romantic gesture she'd ever experienced. Her heart might never slow down.

"I don't deserve it, but I'll take it." Toby wrapped his free arm around her shoulders and pulled her to his side. His chin nuzzled her hair. "From now on, I'll always be there to hold your hand. Got it? Anytime you want me to."

She tucked her head against his chest and carefully

wrapped her arms around him for a prolonged hug. To-morrow she'd reestablish the boundaries that kept them both safe. Because nestled against his heartbeat, it was easy to forget about not wanting to ever date or trust a man again.

Chapter Nine

Even though he was trying to get breakfast on the table as quickly as he could, Toby kept an eye on the staircase for any signs of Jenna. Usually she was the first up. He'd wander into the Crests' house and find her sipping hazelnut coffee out of a gigantic colorful mug in the front room with her dad's Bible draped across her knees.

It had become his favorite sight in the world.

Kasey yawned, flipped her long hair over her shoulder and examined the cards in her hands. "Got a grouper?"

Mr. Crest pursed his lips and lowered his eyebrows as he drew his cards closer to his face. "Looks like you're going to have to go fish."

"A lobster?" she asked.

"Kase." Toby used a spatula to point at her. "Play by the rules, or don't play at all."

"Now, that's a different story. I do have one of those." Mr. Crest pushed the card with a happy dancing cartoon lobster on it across the table to her.

"Thanks, Mr. Crest." She snatched it up and laid down her match. "You're a pal."

Toby turned back to the stovetop, shaking his head. Mr. Crest had become the quintessential indulgent grandpa, but Toby didn't step in and make Kasey give the card back even though the fair way to play was for them to alternate asking about fish instead of Kasey getting to take two turns in a row. Those two had worked out a bond that he wasn't about to infringe on. However, after witnessing Kasey lose it over his falling off the ladder yesterday, Toby knew it was time to sit down with Mr. Crest and Jenna and discuss what would become of Kasey if something ever did happen to him. The retirement facility in Florida where his parents lived didn't allow children, and Sophia's parents had both succumbed to health issues over the course of the last five years. Kasey's father had abandoned Sophia while she was pregnant and given away his paternal rights, refusing to even meet his daughter.

Toby's free hand fisted at his side. How could a man do that? So far, he'd had Kasey in his care for five months. The first four and a half had been spent at the apartment Kasey had grown up in, packing things up, saying goodbye to that life and grieving, and the last few weeks had been spent with the Crests. Toby loved Kasey. Loved her as if she were his own child and felt fiercely protective over her. It was her father's loss. The man was like some pirate who had struck priceless treasure, buried it and forgotten about it when he went out sailing.

Would the Crests agree to be named as guardians when he wrote a will? Or would that be asking too much, too soon? Taking on the task of raising a child was a big deal—a lifelong one. And Jenna already had a lot on her plate with her father's condition.

He broke a couple more eggs into the glass bowl. "How many do you think Jenna will eat?"

Mr. Crest swiveled in his chair. "Are you going to make bacon, too?"

"Scrambled eggs are nothing without bacon." Toby poured cream into the eggs.

Kasey wiggled in her seat. "Do you make runny ones? I don't like runny ones."

"No, my dear." He cracked his knuckles and stretched, playing up that it was all part of serious egg preparation. "I make excellent scrambled eggs. I know all the secrets."

"Hold on." She braced her hands on the table, her eyes widening. "There are secrets. Tell me."

"Secret number one." Toby held up the bowl. "Whip them a lot. Getting air into the mix makes them fluffy. Secret number two." He turned on the burner. "Take the pan off the heat before they're fully cooked. They keep cooking on their own—even when they're on the plate—and that keeps them from getting rubbery."

Mr. Crest scooped all the cards off the table and shuffled them back into the Go Fish box. "It's safe to say I'll never question your cooking abilities again."

Toby chuckled. "I wouldn't go that far."

Kasey dropped her chin into her hand. "Jenna probably ate already."

Toby sprinkled salt and pepper into the egg batter. "Honey, she couldn't have eaten. She's not up yet."

Mr. Crest nodded. "She was out at the barn kitchen until late. I don't know how late, because she was still in there baking when I went to bed around midnight. We should let her sleep in as long as her body needs. I can manage the store."

"You're not listening to me." Kasey raised her voice. "She's up. I know she is because she's not in her room. I checked her bedroom before I came down. Her bed was made and everything."

She hadn't slept in her bed? But then where was she?

The whisk stilled in Toby's hand. He clicked off the burner on the oven and turned around.

Mr. Crest motioned for him to skedaddle. "Go check, son. If my legs worked right, I'd be up those stairs already. You have my permission."

Toby took the steps two at a time and flung open the door to Jenna's room. Empty. No clothes on the ground, and Kasey was right, the bed didn't even look slept in. He pounded back down the stairs. "She's not there. I'm going to check the kitchen and shop."

Her dad wrung his hands and looked off toward the door. "If you don't find her there, start searching the property. This isn't like her."

Toby pointed at Kasey. "Stay here."

He flung open the back door and jogged to the barn that housed the shop and industrial kitchen, passing Jenna's car along the way. In fact, all the vehicles were accounted for. He fumbled with the knob to the front door of the shop before successfully making it inside. It was empty, too.

"Please be in the kitchen." He shoved through the heavy door that separated the two areas. Flour dusted the middle island, a mountain of fresh baked goods littered the countertops, and the air smelled like cinnamon and caramel. But no Jenna.

He jogged back outside and scanned the area around the house. "Where are you?"

Toby kept a fast clip as he made his way into the

orchard. There were benches and picnic tables spread across the property for customers to use when they visited. With so many acres making up the Crests' land, she could literally be anywhere. He was halfway through the rows of trees when it hit him that he should have grabbed the golf cart. But he couldn't think straight. Going back now would cost him time, and she could be just around the next bend or the one after that.

She was okay, right? She'd probably just gone for a walk. And not slept. And...

He stumbled and had to grab on to a low-hanging limb to keep his feet on the ground. *Slow down.* Worry was making him clumsy, and clumsy could cause him to miss a clue.

If something had happened to her—

"God? Help me find her. Please? This is probably nothing." He swallowed hard, more emotion coating his words than he'd realized was there. "But Jenna means a lot to me. I think we both know she always has."

He stepped over the deer fencing and ventured out into the wooded part of the Crest property. Mr. Crest had always talked about expanding the orchard out into the wild areas they owned, but even when they were children, Jenna had begged him to keep the woods as they were. It looked like Jenna had won that battle. Toby passed the site of their old clubhouse. A part of the structure was still up in the trees, but it looked rotted through. She wasn't up there.

"Jenna!" he called.

He circled back toward the small pond located on the edge of the property. When he'd started his search, he hadn't figured it would take this long. He was sure he'd find her out already picking apples, and they'd laugh about her starting the day so early. Or at one of the picnic tables with her Bible, wanting to enjoy the fresh morning air. But it seemed she was simply…gone.

Toby had known life with Jenna again for only a few weeks, and just the thought that he wouldn't get to spend some time with her this morning was causing his heart to pound frantically against his rib cage.

But she was okay. She had to be.

He brushed through the last of the tree line and scanned the area by the pond. *There.* Curled on a bench swing built to face the pond, with a blanket tucked around her, Jenna looked like she was asleep. The swing slowly rocked her in the chilly morning breeze. Toby braced his hand on a nearby tree, only now noticing that he was out of breath and his limbs were shaky. The place where he'd injured his knee in that game, years ago, ached, too. But none of that mattered.

She was safe. She was fine.

"Thank you," he whispered before rounding the bench to stand in front of it. He studied her for a moment, sunlight traced over her eyelashes, making her blond hair shine. His heart squeezed with a warm flush of relief and something else. And there, as morning light poured over them, realization hit Toby as hard as a linebacker tackling him.

He was in love with Jenna Crest.

Not just because she was beautiful—which she was. Far more than attraction gave her a place in his heart. Jenna was kind, encouraging and hardworking. He became someone he liked when Jenna was around—she brought out Toby's best. Despite the fact that she knew the worst about him, she'd still sat on the couch beside him yesterday, hugging him. A good day in his book included charming a smile out of her, and a great day was one when he made her laugh. It was possible he'd always been in love with her and had been too stupid to acknowledge it.

While he wanted to stand there pondering his revelation, he realized that would be selfish. He had to get her back to her father's house—Mr. Crest and Kasey would be worried.

Toby dropped down to one knee and rested his hands on the edge of the bench to stop it from rocking in the wind. "Jenna," he whispered. "Hey, sweetheart, you need to wake up."

She moaned and rolled over so her back was to him. "So tired. Just...fell...to...sleep."

Had she pulled an all-nighter in the kitchen? She should have told him. He would have stayed up and helped. He wasn't much of a baker, but he would happily give up a night of rest to spend time with her.

Wow, and he'd *just* realized he was in love.

Man...he was slow.

He peeled back the dew-coated blanket and then leaned and lifted her arm so it wrapped over his neck. He tucked one of his arms under her knees and another behind her back and picked her up. Jenna's body curved into his automatically, her head dropping against the place where his shoulder and chest met. Sweet scents of everything she'd baked drifted over them. She still had her eyes closed, but her arms tightened around him to connect in a loop around his neck as he carried her, letting him know she wasn't fully asleep.

"You can relax. I got you." He kept his voice quiet and tried to control his emotions. As puffs of her breath landed on his neck and her curls swayed back and forth over his arm, it took all of the self-control he possessed not to bend down and kiss her.

"You came," she whispered.

He glanced down. Her eyes were still closed. Was she awake? Or talking in her sleep?

It didn't matter. Now that he knew he loved this woman, he'd speak the truth, even when it scared him. "I'll always come for you. I've let you down in the past, but I won't again."

Her head drooped against his chest. She rubbed her cheek against his heartbeat, as if she was rooting around for warmth or simply enjoyed the sound.

Toby swallowed hard.

His knee throbbed, but he continued down between two rows of trees in the orchard. In this area, the trees' branches still hung heavy with apples. He'd need to focus the team on harvesting this portion of the orchard today.

Jenna sighed. "I always thought…"

"You always thought what?" He ducked under a low-hanging limb.

"Our wedding…here…the…orchard."

Toby stopped walking and looked down at her. She had to be asleep. Especially with the stilted way she was talking.

Our wedding.

At some point in her life, she'd thought about marrying him?

He shouldn't… Maybe it was terrible, but he couldn't help himself from asking questions.

He tightened his hold on her and started moving again. "When we get married, you wanted to have the wedding in the orchard?"

She nodded against him. His treacherous heart, pounding out a double-time march in his chest, was bound to wake her up.

So, she'd thought about getting married when they were teens? Or thought it now? "When?"

"Spring's…nice."

The season was not the answer he was looking for.

But he'd play along. That was the right thing to do when someone was sleep-talking, right? Play along as to not alarm them? "It is. With all the trees blooming."

"Mmm-hmm."

He licked his lips. "What about fall? This season. Now?"

"Yes," she whispered. "Now. S'good…too."

Her words rocked through him. Did Jenna love him? *Yes. Now.* Could she, after everything? And if she did, what did that mean for them? For Kasey and her father?

As they exited the orchard, Kasey came running outside. "You found her!"

"Shh. She's sleeping," Toby hushed her. "You were supposed to stay with Mr. Crest."

"He told me to keep watch from the porch. Said you might need help." Her green eyes were deep and scanning Jenna, as if she was expecting to find an injury. Kasey had been worried, too.

"Okay. Grab the doors, then come with me all the way up to her room, all right?"

Kasey held the back door, and Toby carried Jenna inside. Mr. Crest spotted them and looked at Toby. Something passed between them—understanding of the mutual love they had for the woman in his arms— and then Mr. Crest nodded. "Take her up."

Toby used his head to motion toward the stairs, silently telling Kasey to go in front of him. She caught the hint and pounded up the steps. It was a wonder that Jenna didn't wake up with all the racket the small girl was making.

Kasey eased open the door to Jenna's room and ran to the bed. She flung back the blankets. "I'm ready." Kasey grinned. "I'll tuck her in."

"Whisper," Toby reminded her. He lay down his precious cargo and froze for a second. He wanted to drop a kiss to her temple, but not yet. Not without Jenna's knowledge and consent, and definitely not in front of Kasey, who would never stop talking about the show of affection.

But if he hung around too much longer, he might not be able to hold back. At the moment, he didn't trust himself not to shake Jenna awake so he could profess his love to her. Good thing Kasey was around. Her presence helped him keep his wits together.

He fled down the stairs and offered a quick explanation to Mr. Crest before leaving the house without eating breakfast. Toby headed into the orchard to work, but his thoughts kept drifting to images of his best friend in a white dress walking toward him down the long, natural aisle made of trees.

Blazes of sunlight dappled the walls of Jenna's childhood bedroom. She stretched and turned, trying to will her eyes to focus on the clock perched on her nightstand, but the red numbers bled together. She blinked a couple times. Her contacts needed more moisture before she was going to be able to see much of anything clearly.

Jenna scrubbed her hand down her face while she yawned. A stretch followed, complete with some popping noises from her spine. Actually, her entire back ached, as if she'd slept on a concrete floor all night.

Or as if her dream last night had been real.

She snuggled back into her blankets and closed her eyes, reliving the inviting image her mind had created of being carried through the orchard in Toby's strong arms. The steady hum of his heartbeat beside her, and the deep smell of cedar that must be from the cologne he wore. Jenna cupped her hand over her cheek, remembering the waffle texture of the black fitted henley he'd been wearing. Toby was funny that way. He always started the day in a henley or sweatshirt, but within ten minutes of working, he'd peel the first layer off and stay in his T-shirt for the rest of the day.

It had been a long time since she'd enjoyed such a detailed dream. After everything happened in college, she'd been afraid of falling asleep and battled insomnia in the beginning. For the first few years, because she wasn't dealing well with the emotional trauma of what she'd been through, her mind had chosen to cope by replaying the attacks each night. She could block out her thoughts during the day, but her mind wasn't safe while sleeping.

But nothing felt safer than the dream she'd experienced last night, than picturing herself in Toby's arms.

Keep dreaming, lady. Because it sure isn't ever going to happen in real life.

Her door eased open, and a little head peeked in. "You're finally awake."

Jenna hauled herself up to a sitting position, propped against the headboard. She patted the bed beside her, inviting Kasey to join her. The little girl sometimes liked to snuggle with Jenna. She'd mentioned that she used to do that with her mom sometimes.

That was all the prompting Kasey required. She launched herself onto the bed, landing with a thud and a rush of air. "I thought you might sleep for-ev-er."

Jenna knocked her shoulder gently into Kasey's. "Guess I overslept."

"By a lot. A whole, whole lot."

Jenna stifled another yawn. "Are they waiting on me for breakfast? I better get cleaned up." She was still wearing what she'd worn yesterday. Lovely. She must have shuffled over from the kitchen last night in a zombielike state and fallen into bed from pure exhaustion. The last time she'd looked at the clock in the kitchen, it had been closing in on four in the morning, and she'd still had pies in the oven. That put her not going to bed until five or later.

Kasey giggled. "It's long past breakfast. Lunch, too."

Jenna swung her head toward the little girl. "Wait. What? It's past noon?" How had she slept so late? She never did that. "Why did you guys let me sleep so long?" She pushed forward as if to get up and caught a look at the clock. It was past one in the afternoon. "The shop."

Kasey caught her arm. "Your friend Kendall stopped by. She wanted to talk to you about using the barn for her wedding. But when we told her you didn't sleep all night, she volunteered to stay and help. Her and Grandpa are down helping people."

Jenna relaxed her shoulders.

Okay, if Kendall was helping Dad, then Jenna could sneak in a quick shower and a bite to eat before heading outside. She patted her hair. It felt big. The joys of having naturally curly hair.

Kasey swung her feet so they banged against the bed-frame. "I came in to get a cheese stick for a snack. They said to leave you alone, but I just had to check on you. After Toby brought you back, I was so worried. I wanted to make sure you were okay. You don't have a cold from sleeping outside, do you? I don't want you to get sick."

Jenna's world came to a screeching halt. She grabbed the metal rod that ran over the top of her headrest, try-ing to ground herself. "I'm sorry, after Toby what?"

"You weren't in your room this morning. I checked." Kasey's eyes were huge as she spoke. Excitement pulsed from her words. "Toby went to look for you. He carried you all the way back here. He's pretty strong, isn't he?"

Her dream. No. No. No. That was real? He'd carried her, and she'd babbled about wanting to marry him? Jenna dropped her head into her hands and took a few deep breaths. Then she turned toward Kasey. "I was outside? In the orchard? Toby carried me? You're sure? Absolutely sure?"

"Uh-huh." *Thud. Thud. Thud.* Her feet hit the bed-frame with pendulum precision.

"It was all real? All of it?"

Kasey's nods were exaggerated. "I saw."

Acid pooled in the back of Jenna's mouth. She was going to be sick. "This can't be happening." Jenna curved her shoulders inward and rocked back and forth. "I'll never be able to face him again."

"Jenna?" Kasey snaked her hand to rest on Jenna's thigh. Jenna stopped rocking and stared down at the contact.

"I was scared," Kasey whispered. "When you weren't here. Just like I was scared yesterday when Toby fell."

Kasey needs you.

*God, help me say the right things to her. Help me
get out of my own head, my own fear. I can't spin into
a panic attack over how embarrassed I am over Toby,
over what happened. God, give me strength. Help me be
a beacon of hope for this child, one that points to You.*

Jenna reached trembling hands to frame the sides of
Kasey's face. "You don't have to be scared. I'm fine. I
think. I'll be fine."

Kasey's eyes searched hers. "You're sure you're not
sick?"

Only if heartsick counts.

Wasting time worrying about the turmoil she felt
concerning Toby wouldn't aid Jenna in calming Kasey's fears. "I was tired and it was so early in the morning I wanted to watch the sunrise. So I went down to
the pond. We—I mean I—used to watch sunsets there
sometimes. I must have fallen asleep."

Kasey latched on to her hand. "I really like you guys.
Toby and your dad and you."

"We love you, too, Kasey." Jenna released Kasey's
hand so she could wrap her arm around the child's shoulders. She pulled Kasey close. "You know that, right?"

"I feel like it's wrong." Kasey studied the toes of her
purple shoes. "I like you guys, but I miss my mom still."
Her voice was so small. "Do you think that's okay?"

"Kasey." Jenna pulled the little girl into a full hug as
her tiny shoulders started shaking with tears. "I lost my
mom, too," Jenna said. "I miss her all the time. It's okay
to miss them. Missing is the heart's memory of love."

"What if I forget her?" Kasey's voice shook.

"We'll make sure you don't." Jenna rubbed a circle into Kasey's back. "Do you know what helped me?
Here." She leaned over, opened the drawer on her night-

stand and pulled out one of the many empty notebooks she'd purchased simply because she liked the design on the outside and relished the idea of writing in them one day. Her journal-purchasing habit was seriously getting out of hand. She'd never fill them all.

Jenna placed the book into Kasey's hands. "This is a journal. I want you to start writing in it."

Kasey ran her thumb over the intricate design on the cover. "About what?"

"You can write down things you remember about your mom. You could draw pictures. You could write what you would tell her about your day if she were still here."

"I like knowing that you knew her." Kasey hugged the journal to her chest and rested her chin on the top of it.

"She was a really fun person. She and I had sleepovers when she used to visit Toby's family during summer break. We'd talk late into the night, right in this room."

"Really?"

Jenna tucked Kasey's long hair behind her ears. "Really."

"Sometimes I feel so mad," she said in a tiny voice, as if she was fearful of admitting it out loud. "Or super, super sad. It's scary—feeling so much. Did that happen to you, too, when your mom died?"

"It did. Sometimes I still struggle with that. But I'm going to tell you a secret. I have a little trick." Jenna hopped off the bed, crossed to her closet and fished a colorful decorated shoebox off the top shelf inside. "See this box?" She carried it back to the bed. "It's an old shoebox that I covered with pictures I cut out of magazines."

"It's pretty."

"All these things on here remind me of my mom." Jenna tapped a picture of a needle and thread. "She used to sew quilts. And she was the best cook." She found an image of a cookie and a chalkboard on her collage artwork. "She was also my teacher. She homeschooled me for most of my life. I don't know if you knew that."

Jenna lifted the top off to reveal all the notecards inside. "But inside this box, that's the good stuff. See, I keep cards near my box and on my nightstand. I write down good memories of her, and I also write down encouraging quotes or positive things that happen in my life. I put them all in this box, and then whenever I'm having a day where I'm struggling with feeling mad or super sad, I open this box and read through all the cards until I feel better. It's a visual way of counting your blessings."

Kasey caressed her fingers over the lid. "I want to make one."

"I'll run to the store today and get you a box and a bunch of magazines so you can decorate it." Jenna put the lid back on, slid off the bed and tucked her box back into the closet.

Kasey scooted to the very edge of the bed. "Do you still put good thoughts in there?"

"I do. And do you know what? I wrote a card about you and put it in this box." Jenna tweaked Kasey's nose.

"You did?"

"I did."

"I want to tell Toby the box idea." Kasey headed for the door. "I'm going to put a card about you in my box, too. Maybe a couple."

After Kasey left, Jenna circled around her room a

few times, contemplating what to do. Maybe she could play off her interaction with Toby. *Oh, I was dreaming it was Brad Pitt carrying me. Not you.* But he'd see right through that. She bit the edge of her nail.

He was never supposed to become aware of her long-hidden feelings. Couldn't they just go on as they had last week? Have fun together. Focus on working together and taking care of Kasey. She didn't want to endure some big letdown with Toby where he detailed why he didn't feel the same way and had to give the awkward "I'm sorry I don't like you like that" speech.

And he wouldn't, because Jenna was going to take a page out of his playbook. She'd ignore the situation. Act like she didn't remember. If he didn't bring it up, she wouldn't either.

Chapter Ten

Toby shot Jenna a look that he hoped she took as one of apology when Kasey captured her hand and tugged. The girl wasn't about to give up on her quest to get the three of them to go on an adventure together. She'd pounced on Jenna the second she was free. It was still long before dinnertime, and Jenna had just closed the Crest Country Store for the day.

Kasey made her eyes look like they belonged on a sad cartoon puppy dog. "Please, please, please. Say you'll pick apples with us." No one could stay strong when it came to the pleading puppy face.

Poor Jenna. She didn't stand a chance.

Then again, it wasn't like he had made any attempt to talk Kasey out of the idea when she'd presented it to him. Time with Jenna and Kasey? No-brainer. Even if his arms ached from working in the orchard all day, he wouldn't skip a chance to make a new memory with his two favorite ladies. Toby leaned his neck to the side, enjoying the stretch. The manual labor he performed in the orchard left him ten times as sore as the hardest football practice. It was far more rewarding, too—in a different way.

Jenna laid her hand over Kasey's and offered her a small smile. "Aw, that does sound fun, but it's been a long day. How about a rain check?"

"You only woke up after lunch. That's not long. That's a short day. Super short." Kasey's eyes got even bigger, and her bottom lip came out in an embellished pout. The kid had talent. He'd give her that. Toby should sign her up for one of the park district's drama classes.

"You know, Kasey has a point," Toby joked in an effort to catch Jenna's gaze, but she seemed to be avoiding all eye contact with him.

Was it because of this morning when he'd carried her? Had she been awake? If so, did she still care about him like that?

He sucked in a steady breath.

Kasey let go of Jenna and threw her arms out at her sides and spun a little. "We live on an orchard. I've lived here for almost a month, and I haven't picked any apples. That's, like, against the law, I think." She stopped spinning to zero in on Jenna. "I haven't seen you pick any either. You need to pick apples."

"It *is* really nice out this afternoon," Toby added.

Jenna finally looked his way, but her eyes darted away before meeting his. A pretty red flush colored her cheeks. Blond curls tumbled around her shoulders and down her back. She wore dark jeans and a lightweight flannel shirt that was open in the front, showing a cream T-shirt and a belt cinching her waste. And high boots encased her calves.

All Toby wanted to do was reach out and pull her and Kasey into his arms—together. Ask if they'd be his family forever. After realizing his feelings for her this morning, he hadn't been able to think of anything besides Jenna all day.

"Please," Kasey insisted. "I'll bug you all night until you say yes."

Jenna popped her hands onto her hips. "Well, when you put it that way, it sounds like I don't have a choice." Her grin gave them their answer.

Kasey whooped. "You want to come! I know you do!"

"All right. You twisted my arm. Let me just go change out of this and—"

Toby caught her arm. After seeing her again, he didn't want to part with her. If they let her head up to her bedroom, she might talk herself out of going with them. Jenna tended to get lost in her head when she was worrying.

He took a step closer and dropped his voice. "You don't need to change. Come on, let's head out."

Kasey danced around them. "I'm going to go get a basket. Should I get a big basket or a small one? I think a medium one. I'm going to get one that won't be too heavy." She dashed off toward the barn, where they stored all the orchard's supplies. Kasey wasn't aware that the Crest property had five or six sheds full of equipment scattered across the property. The biggest one was near an area where Mr. Crest had always kept the hives of bees that pollinated the trees every spring and summer.

Jenna smoothed her free hand down the front of her flannel until she reached the bottom button. Eyes down, she toyed with the edge of the fabric. "I worked in this. The shop gets hot. I'm probably sweaty and have flour on me and—"

Toby walked his fingers up her arm until he reached her shoulder blade. Then he tipped her chin so he could stare into her deep blue eyes. "You look beautiful. You always do, no matter what. You always have. You're the kindest, most honest person I know, and that makes you beautiful every second of every day."

Was it too much? He was having a hard time holding back.

She rolled her eyes and brushed away his fingers. "That sounds an awful lot like how you would describe someone if you were trying to set them up on a blind date. The age-old 'Oh, but she has such a nice personality.'"

Her doubt speared him, but it was his fault. Of course his mistakes during high school would make her second-guess any compliments he paid her. Although she'd offered forgiveness, forgiveness didn't erase memories. It would take patience and repetition and a consistent demonstration of how he felt about her to get Jenna to believe otherwise. He had a long hill to climb, but it was worth it. *She* was worth it. Toby would be faithful and wait for the right time—even though he wanted to spit out "I love you" right then. He would bide his time until he was certain she'd believe those words.

Still, he needed her to know he was being truthful.

Toby stepped even closer, getting into her space. His cheek brushed hers as he whispered right beside her ear. "I'm so attracted to you I can't see straight sometimes. You have no idea how—"

"I got the basket!" Kasey burst between them and held a small bucket aloft. "We can head out now."

Jenna tucked her hair back behind her ears. She looked at Toby, then looked away, looked at Kasey, and then her gaze strayed back to Toby. A blush spread down her neck and warmed her cheeks. She bit her cheek on one side, studying him as if he were a science-fair project. Toby met her scrutiny.

Believe it, Jenna. I meant every word and more.

Kasey let the basket dangle beside her. Her eyes narrowed. "Something silly is going on here. You two are looking all funny at each other. Were you telling secrets? Can I hear?"

"Apples." Jenna grabbed Kasey's shoulders and steered the girl toward the orchard. "Let's go pick apples."

Kasey dropped back to slip her free hand into Jenna's. She handed the pail to Toby and then took hold of his hand, too, so she was skipping in between them. "Jenna? Is Toby your boyfriend?"

Jenna coughed and sputtered for air. "Girls and guys can just be friends."

"I know, but Toby's great and you're great, so..."

Toby squeezed Kasey's hand. "Kase, don't pester. Focus on picking apples, and think about all the things we'll make with them."

"Mmm." Kasey used their arms as leverage to hop over a downed branch. "We could make those baked ones again. Or the turnovers. The apple butter is good, too. Oh, but the fritters are my favorite. No, wait. I take that back. I forgot about caramel apples."

"What about cider donuts?" Toby asked.

Kasey gave a dramatic groan. "Everything. Everything apple wins."

They headed toward the side of the orchard to the trees holding the last Gravenstein apples of the season. Gravensteins were early bloomers and would all fall from their limbs by next week. They needed to focus on clearing the last of those before picking from trees with apples that would hold into next month.

Jenna pointed to the first tree in the line. "This one looks good."

Toby hauled Kasey onto his shoulders so she could reach the branches.

"Be careful up there." Jenna inched closer with the basket propped on her hip.

Toby and Kasey picked the apples, then passed them to Jenna. They made a great team.

Why hadn't he realized how he felt about Jenna years ago? It would have alleviated so much of his stumbling through life. For so long, he'd blocked out love. How stupid. All because he'd been afraid of losing people like he'd lost Ben, and his parents after Ben's death. Sure, he'd successfully prevented all the bad emotions, the hard things, from penetrating his heart, but the blockades had kept out the good stuff, too.

He glanced over at Jenna and Kasey.

The best stuff.

He wouldn't live like that any longer—not now, when he knew what he'd missed out on. Toby could be braver than that—he'd open up, even if that meant losing sometimes. Even if it meant people deciding they didn't like him. Even if it meant flat-out rejection.

On the way back home Kasey ran ahead of them, excited to poll Mr. Crest on what they should use all the apples for tonight. Toby lugged the overloaded pail under his arm while Jenna walked a few feet away, glancing over her shoulder toward the setting sun.

Toby cleared his throat. "I really enjoy spending time with you."

She offered him a gentle smile. "I'm glad you're back. This place is better when you're around. I can't take care of it the way you do."

He reached over, took her hand and laced their fingers together. And she didn't pull away.

Jenna drew her cardigan tighter around herself, crossed her arms and shoved her fists into her armpits as she pressed farther into the darkness. Years ago, she'd been fond of nighttime walks. Strolling under the stars used to do wonders to clear her head. Without fear, she used to prowl the rows of trees, praying late into the evening. There had been no need to worry about waking up at a certain time the next day because Mom liked to start the homeschool lessons later anyway.

For almost eight years now, nighttime had no longer been safe. Ross had robbed her of that. He'd robbed her of so much more than the obvious. Her last evening stroll had been the final day of summer before her sophomore year of college.

Jenna shivered.

Autumn nights near Lake Michigan were bound to be cold. She should have tossed on a fleece jacket before stepping out, but she wouldn't go back for it now. Jenna cut into the orchard, following the same path she, Toby and Kasey had taken to pick apples earlier.

Inside, she couldn't think straight. Not with Kasey and Toby hanging out with Dad in the front room. How could she work through her jumble of emotions concerning Toby when he was nearby? She'd slipped out the back door, telling herself she'd be quick.

Weeks ago when Toby arrived, she'd wanted him

gone. Now she didn't know if she could ever handle him leaving. How did that kind of flip happen?

Because you never stopped loving him.

She pressed her hand to her cheek, remembering the rub of his stubble and the warmth of his breath as he whispered flirtatious words. If only she could cherish how he treated her today, but she couldn't lie to herself. Toby didn't care about her beyond friendship. No matter what he said or did. When they were younger, he'd been the same way, and it had meant nothing. His behavior had changed because of the sleepy words she'd muttered when he carried her from the pond.

Was Toby messing with her?

Jenna swallowed hard. How was she supposed to protect her heart from him? It screamed to be handed over to him every time they were together. But she couldn't do that—not fully—because she knew deep down that in the end he'd decide she wasn't good enough for him, like he'd done in the past. Someday when he left, taking Kasey with him—because there was no possible way he'd stay here forever—he'd leave Jenna's heart in the dirt again.

Something rustled along the deer fencing to her right. Jenna froze. She tilted her head, listening for any minuscule movements in the bushes beyond the low fence. A steady thump of footsteps coming from the orchard set her on edge.

What made her think she was safe out here? Goose Harbor enjoyed a low crime rate, but the orchard sat on the far edge of town, just a few streets off the highway. Anyone could come onto their property without the Crests noticing. Once, Dad had located a homeless man living in their woods, eating the apples.

No one in the house would hear if she cried out.

She was alone. Unprotected.

Easy prey.

Jenna stumbled backward as terror closed around her dry throat. She blinked against the night, silent tears rolling down her cheeks.

She hated feeling so vulnerable.

Willing her legs to move, Jenna took off blindly through the nearest row of trees. She pushed forward, grabbing branches. Something or someone else tromped along the cold earth not far away.

Escape. Get away.

Deep gasps of breath heaved from her lips as she rounded another row of trees and sprinted deeper into the orchard. Kicking over fallen apples, she stumbled. Someone called her name. A man.

Ross had known her name, and that hadn't meant she was safe.

Keep going. Don't stop.

Tripping again, Jenna tore out of the orchard and rushed onward. The dim, silver splash of moonlight cast everything in terrifying shadows. Air whooshed out of her stomach as she smacked into something hard. It wobbled and crashed to the ground beside her. A hive. She clawed forward. The deep hum of angry bugs, awoken from their slumber, reverberated in her ears. If she was near Dad's bees, one of their toolsheds wasn't far. Jenna sprang to her feet, batting at the irate but sleepy bees.

Spotting the shed, she hurried forward. Her breath burned in her throat, and her thoughts pounded an assault against her emotions. What if the man found her… caught her…kept coming after her no matter what? Not again. She couldn't take it. Never again.

If she couldn't outrun him, she'd hide. And if he found her, she'd fight. This time she wouldn't go easily. This time she'd choose strength.

Jenna tugged open the heavy metal door and hurled herself into the toolshed. She tore toward the back of the deep structure and burrowed herself amid the equipment. Her hands scraped against rakes and hoes, but the pain let her know she was still alive. Breathing. Fighting. Along the back wall, Jenna dropped to her knees, curled into a ball and threw her arms over her head and neck.

She tried to cry silently, jamming her face into her legs to muffle any sounds. But no matter how much she attempted to push the memories away, she was a sophomore in college again. Crouched down, trying to hide from Ross and the power drunkenness gave him. But he always found her. His rough hands were always ready for her.

"Oh, God, help me. Protect me." Jenna shivered.

With a loud clank, the heavy door burst open. Maybe she could spring forward, grab a weapon and fend off whoever it was. Then again, if she stayed still, maybe she wouldn't have to. The darkness worked in her favor. She'd be difficult to see hidden within the clutter of tools stored in the shed. Jenna huddled, pressing herself tighter against the wall.

Make me invisible.

"Jenna?" A tender, tentative voice sounded in the darkness. "You in here?"

A trick. Ross once said he was hurt and needed help to get her to open the door. She'd fallen for it and wasn't going to make that mistake again.

Footsteps thumped against the wooden floor and came near her. Jenna held her breath. A hand skimmed her back, and terror gripped her. She uncurled herself and shoved at the man with all her power. She spun and grabbed a rake from a hook off the wall; then she thrust it between them. "Don't touch me."

Cloaked in shadows, the man held up his hands in surrender. "You're scaring me, Jenna. What's going on? I want to help." He took a step forward, but she met his movement with a jab in his direction.

"I won't let you hurt me," Jenna ground out.

"Jenna. Sweetheart. Put the rake down." The man's voice, bathed in warmth, reached through her panic, and she finally recognized it. "It's Toby. No one's going to hurt you on my watch."

"Toby." Her shoulders sagged with relief. "I'm sorry... I thought... I thought..." Her weapon clattered to the ground and she dropped to her knees. The aftertaste of fear pulsed tension through her muscles, but her mind was back under control. She hadn't battled an attack that strong in months.

Toby came to his knees in front of her, pulling Jenna to his chest without hesitating. She fisted her hands into the soft fabric of his T-shirt, shoved her forehead into his sternum and broke into ugly, shoulder-shaking sobs. She cried so hard she could hardly catch her breath. But hanging on to him helped ground her in reality.

"It's you," she kept repeating. "I'm glad it's you."

He slowly scooted back toward the open doorway with Jenna in his arms. Fresh air hit her like a slap, but she welcomed the chill. Anything to help her focus.

There's no danger. I'm safe.

Toby ran his hand over her hair and cupped the back of her head. "Please tell me what's going on. Help me understand. I said my name. Said your name. But it's like you couldn't hear me. You just took off."

Jenna closed her eyes and absorbed the scent of him—cedar and sweat and sweetness from constantly handling the apples, herbs lingering from dinner—home base. Her safe harbor.

She fought a losing battle against the trembles that kept working up her spine. What was wrong? What had happened? Why was she running? "He raped me."

The muscles crisscrossing Toby's chest tensed. He set her back a foot away from his body. A sliver of moonlight showed his nostrils flared, his jaw clenched, his eyes hard. Shame plunked into her stomach like a heavy rock. He'd never think the same about her. She should have kept things—

"Who?" he growled. "When? Is he here?" He took a labored breath like a runner after a marathon, his whole chest heaving. "Nearby? I'll—"

"Oh, wow. You thought…" Jenna pushed her palms into his chest. "Tobe. I'm fine. It was a long time ago."

Air rattled out of him. He placed a hand over the top of hers. "I'm so sorry. Is that what…"

Caused you to clam up? Made you constantly scared? Started your anxiety?

His question could have ended with any of those, but they all had the same answer.

She nodded. "Sophomore year of college."

He sat back on his heels. "The year you quit. That's why. Your dad doesn't know?"

"No. And please, promise you won't tell him. I couldn't bear him knowing. He'd feel responsible in some way—I know it would hurt him, and I can't handle bringing him down. Promise me?"

Toby closed his eyes as if making the promise bothered him, but he nodded once.

"I was dating him." She puffed out a lungful of air. "At first, I thought it was my fault."

"Jenna." Ah. There it was. The upset way Toby said her name when she belittled herself.

She shrugged. "The girls on my floor told me it was normal—that I should want to—and I was overreacting. He was my first—well, the only boyfriend I've ever had."

Toby worked his jaw back and forth. "That doesn't mean he's allowed to do whatever he wants." He picked up her hand and held on tightly.

"I know that now," she whispered. "I changed myself a lot, after what happened in high school."

His frown deepened. "After I was a jerk?"

"It's stupid." She ran the toe of her tennis shoes back and forth over the long grass just outside the shed.

"Tell me." Toby squeezed her hand. "Please? Unless it's too difficult."

It *shouldn't* be difficult. She'd been through two different counselors and had even attended group therapy sessions in Grand Rapids. Why couldn't she move on like so many of the other women she had met had been able to?

"It's been almost eight years." For a long time, she'd foolishly blamed Toby for her problems. He'd been the catalyst—the old, frumpy Jenna wouldn't have caught Ross's attention. "After graduation I drove to a spa in Grand Rapids and paid a lot of money for a makeover, and I bought all new clothes. When I got to school, I pretended to be outgoing. I went to parties. I hung out with the football team. Ross was on the team. A linebacker."

"I feel sick." Toby rocked forward, hooking his free elbow onto his knee. He rested his head in his hand. "They're huge."

"He was," Jenna continued. "And when he got drunk… I had no chance. I think he thought it was his right. That's what he said. I started hiding from him, but he'd find me. He bribed my roommate to borrow keys to our room. The last time—"

He turned his head to look at her. "How many times?"

"It was five times before I ran away."

Toby scooted closer and laid his hand on her knee. "I'm so sorry that happened to you." His arm went rigid. "Is this okay? Me touching you? I do it all the time without asking. I shouldn't." He let go of her hand and moved his other hand from her leg. "I didn't even think… Does that bother you?"

He looked so worried. As if he thought he might break her.

But really, Toby's contact made her feel cherished. When he looked at her in his special way or reached out to her, it made her forget that she was damaged goods. And while this was her perfect opportunity to set some boundaries for the sake of her heart, she couldn't do it. Not if it meant never holding Toby's hand again. Not when she needed the hug and comfort he'd readily offer.

She grabbed his shirt and tugged him closer. Wrapping her arms around his middle, she rested her head on his chest again. "It doesn't bother me at all. Not with you."

No one besides medical professionals knew the rest, but the safety she found in Toby's arms unglued her tongue. "Once I came home, I found out I was pregnant. I didn't want it. Tobe, I was so scared, but it was wrong for me to wish a life away. I think it was a sin to feel that way." Which was why God had been silent with her ever since.

"Jenna, no."

She squeezed her eyes shut and pushed the side of her face into his chest, as if she could block out the worst. "I lost it—I had a miscarriage—close to the thirteen-week mark. It was worse than what Ross did. That baby died, Toby. My baby died because I hadn't wanted it."

"That's not true." His arms encircled her, and his chin moved against the side of her head. He spoke in a hushed but insistent tone. "Believe me. It's not your fault that your child didn't make it. Don't carry that guilt." He took hold of her arms and set her back a foot from his face. "Sweetheart, look at me." She did. "That guilt's not yours to carry. Okay? It tears me in two to know all that happened to you. To know I played a part in it." He shook his head. "You should have never experienced that. Any of it."

"But I did."

"And not one part of it was your fault. Only—I can't even say his name—only *he* shoulders blame. This is his sin."

"It may be his sin, but it destroyed my life." She laid her hand on her chest. Tears edged her voice, making it raw and shaky. "It destroyed any hope that I'll ever be able to trust a man again. It destroyed my faith in God, Tobe. I prayed. I called out to God, and He didn't stop it." More tears slipped down her cheeks. "He didn't protect me."

"I don't know what to say. But I'm here for you." He reached over and held the side of her face, his thumb tracing it to catch her tears. "Know that. I'm here for you as long as you want me to be."

She leaned into his hand, wanting the affection to be real. Wanting it to mean something more than a friend soothing an old friend.

Toby licked his lips. "I've done things to lose your trust, so I know I can't ask you to have faith in me. But let me try to prove to you that I'm here for the long haul, okay? Can you do that much?"

"I know you're my friend. I'm sorry I pushed you away at first."

"You had every reason to." He climbed out of the shed and held out a hand to her. "Come on. Let's get you home."

When she reached solid ground, he held her around the waist because her legs had turned to applesauce. Knowing that she had nothing to fear was very different from convincing her body she was fine. Attacks always left her feeling spent. If he offered to carry her, she'd say yes and sag against him.

She clung to his side, no doubt stretching out his shirt more. He just pulled her closer as if he didn't mind.

"I won't let anyone hurt you," Toby said. "Not ever again. Not as long as I'm here."

Except she couldn't hold on to his promise, no matter how kindly he offered it, because *he* was the most probable reason for future pain. Losing the only man Jenna had ever loved was bound to hurt far more than anything else in her life to date. Oh, Toby might not be planning to leave, but he would. Someone would catch his eye—his heart.

Someone who wasn't named Jenna Crest.

Chapter Eleven

Toby swirled his coffee around and around in his cup. Come two o'clock, he'd be kicking himself for waking up so early. He stifled a yawn when Jenna crossed through the doorway into the front room of the Crests' house.

She let out a little "Eep," her hand flying to her heart. "You startled me."

He set down his mug. "Sorry. Couldn't sleep."

She rolled her shoulders. "Me neither."

"Come here." He patted the space next to him on the couch.

Normally he strolled into the house in the morning and found her in one of the side chairs reading a Bible, but today he wanted to share with her what he'd learned. After they'd talked last night, Toby had spent hours poring over his Bible and praying for Jenna. He'd asked God for wisdom, too. What hope could he offer someone who didn't believe God responded to calls for help from His followers?

Jenna slowly came around the coffee table and took the seat he offered. Her fingers hugged her own cup of coffee. She jerked her chin to indicate the Bible and handful of colored notecards spread across the table. "What have you got there?"

He gathered them up and waited for her to put down her cup. Then he handed her the stack. "Verses." He cleared his throat. Why was he so nervous? "For you."

As she flipped through them, scanning each verse, she started blinking like crazy. Oh, no. Was she crying? He was trying to help. Not cause her more troubles.

"Jenna, I—"

She met his gaze and held it. "This is the sweetest thing."

Looking into Jenna's misted-over eyes was the wrong move. A sudden desire to lean in and brush his lips against hers almost overwhelmed him. After what had happened with his parents and Ben, Toby had made a choice not to fall in love. But with Jenna, that proved impossible. Besides, she decimated every single one of the reasons he had for not wanting to date. She knew his worst and still cared about him. She stuck with him and believed the best about him, even though he'd disappointed her in the past. She'd endured terrible things in her life and still laughed and joked with him and Kasey. She loved family—loved deeply. Any pain he faced in the future was worth loving this woman.

And she was only inches away.

Toby rocked back, breaking eye contact. After what she shared last night, he didn't feel right planting a kiss on her without some encouragement on her part. He should probably wait for her to make a move or tell him that's what she wanted. Any physical advances ran the risk of scaring her. He could wait. He would wait and win her heart.

He ran his hand down the back of his bed head. "It's just some verses I looked up for you. Hopefully something to encourage you with the stuff you're dealing with."

"'Our Lord and our God, You are my mighty rock, my fortress, my protector.'" She traced her finger down his block lettering on the card. "I want to believe that," she whispered.

I'm so bad at this. Give me words.

"Why don't you?"

"Like I said last night, God never rose to protect me against what happened. I did what the Bible says to do. I cried out to Him, and it didn't matter. It was like He didn't even care."

Toby took her trembling hand in both of his. "Being a Christian doesn't mean nothing bad will ever happen to us. There will always be bad people, evil, sickness— stuff we can't control. God isn't a magic pill that makes everything perfect, and He never promised to take away troubles."

She pushed her palm into his. "Then why bother?"

"He promised to *be with us* during the worst. That makes all the difference."

She snatched her hand out of his, pushed the Bible away. "It's not that easy."

Toby was ruining this opportunity, wasn't he? Failing God.

God, help me.

He'd have to be gut-level honest with her. Let her know that he struggled with this idea as much as she did. "With everything in me, I wish God had stepped in and stopped what happened to you. I wish He saved your mom. Saved Ben. Prevented your dad from getting sick. But He didn't do any of those things." Toby sighed. "Still, I have to believe that God cares. I have to cling to the knowledge that God is upset by every single injustice and that He will make all things right in the end. I have to trust that, because if I don't, then all hope would be lost. I think... I think that's what it means to have faith."

"I know you've suffered, too. I don't mean to make light of the things that have happened in your life. And not just with Ben, but the depression you fought and the career that got taken from you." She slipped her hand over his. "More and more, I want to depend on God and believe what you're saying. I just don't know how to get there. If I knew how, I'd do it, but I feel like I'm behind a wall or something, stuck. I've been stuck in the same place spiritually for eight years."

"You need to realize that you are not your circumstances or your past."

"Toby, don't you see? That's just it, though. Because of what happened to me, I'm damaged. Forever." She studied her coffee and said in a voice he could hardly hear, "I can't change that."

"First off, get that notion out of your head. You are not damaged goods, Jenna Crest. Hear me. Believe that. Okay?" He waited until her eyes met his, and then he added tenderly, "No man in his right mind would see you that way. You are pure and innocent and worth the effort of working through all that."

Her eyebrows rose. She looked hopeful. "Really?"

"Stuff happens in everyone's life. The thing that dictates who you are all depends on *who* you run to for help." He tapped the Bible. "I know you're a Christian, but did you ever give over all that pain to Him, or are you hanging on to it, too afraid to trust what He needs to do in your life in order to heal you? Have you surrendered it?"

"Surrender?" She ran her fingers over her forehead. "But how's that any different from being a Christian? I'm not being snarky—I honestly don't understand."

"When you surrender, you stop trying to protect yourself and leave room for Him to work in your life." His own words rocked through his heart. Did Toby believe that? The Toby a month ago hadn't. But he found he did. Today, he did. "It's an everyday battle of giving over what you want to Him. Each and every day choosing to surrender, and it's not easy."

He failed at it. Daily. But he would make a point to surrender all to God going forward, including his feelings for Jenna.

She started to talk, but he cut her off. "Hear me out. I want you to know that when that bad stuff happened to you, God cared. You didn't see Him, but believe me— He grieved over what happened to you. Evil breaks the heart of God, Jenna. Every time you're scared and huddling somewhere, when your mind is taking you back to those attacks, He's there with you. He's angry about what happened to you, too."

The sound of Mr. Crest's wheelchair made them both swivel toward the doorway. Mr. Crest smiled as wide as a kid discovering a pile of birthday gifts. "Well, don't you two look cozy this morning?"

Toby picked up his cup and got to his feet. "Actually, I was just heading out."

Jenna slipped her hand into his and gave a little tug. "Stay. You'll miss breakfast."

"I would love to, but there's something I need to work

on." He headed out of the house through the kitchen, placing his mug into the dishwasher before he left.

Yesterday evening, before he went searching for Jenna, he'd run through his plan to surprise her with her father, getting Mr. Crest's approval first. Mr. Crest had promised to see Kasey out of the house every morning if Toby needed to use that time to work. They couldn't tell Jenna about his special project, but she would find out soon enough.

And hopefully when she did, she'd understand what it meant.

"Okay, Tobe...when can I take this blindfold off?"

He just chuckled. The rat.

Although, Jenna had to hand it to him—with one of his hands on her lower back guiding her and the other serving as a scratching post for her hands, he'd expertly steered her through the yard without stumbling. He didn't even whimper when she sank her nails into his arm.

Two weeks had passed since the night in the shed when she'd told Toby everything. Two weeks of finding him in the front room reading his Bible when she woke up. Two weeks of his leaving for work early and heading back out to the orchard when he returned from football practice. She'd questioned him again and again about the project that was taking up so much of his time, but he hadn't given her a clue, and he'd made her promise she wouldn't go searching in the orchard to figure it out either.

The Crest Country Store was selling out every weekend. Thankfully, all the seasonal employees were back. They'd enjoyed a boom of pick-your-own-apples business, as well. Also, Jason Moss had accepted six articles from her for publication in the town's newspaper. It was only Goose Harbor, but it was still writing. Ever since that morning when Toby had first joined her in the front room, she'd memorized all the verses he'd written out for her, and they'd slowly started to change her perspective. She wasn't alone. She'd never been alone. Never would be.

God had promised to see her through every moment of her life, if only she'd surrender. He was doing something in Jenna's life—changing her, allowing her to see a new path. One that included the man she was currently clinging to.

"Almost there." Toby's voice was right at her shoulder.

"You know, normal people celebrate birthdays with a cake or balloons," Jenna teased. "A little singing, maybe."

"Ah, but there's the issue—you're not a normal person. Not to me." He gently turned her in a different direction. "So a normal celebration won't do."

"So you're saying I'm abnormal?" she baited him.

"Haven't you heard? All the best people are. Now stand here." He took her shoulders and positioned her. "I hope you like it."

Her blindfold fell away to reveal that she was standing in the forested area of their property where Jenna and Toby's old clubhouse used to be. The old structure had long rotted out, and Jenna had stopped visiting their special place soon after she and Toby stopped speaking.

But the clubhouse was back, and it was bigger. Much bigger.

The top section looked like a functional cabin. It had

a red front door, cute little windows and a wraparound balcony. The space was easily tall enough for an adult to stand inside. Below the cabin area was a second, lower level—an open-air platform area housed a table and tree-stump stools, and seven glass jars hung from the ceiling over the table with flickering candles burning in them. It looked like something out of a children's fairy-tale book.

"You rebuilt our tree house? I can't believe you did this. Tobe, I—" Jenna's voice trembled, and she couldn't continue speaking. She brought her hand to her mouth and let her shoulders shake.

Toby's proud grin dissolved. "You hate it."

"I love it. I'm crying because I love it." She looped her arms around his middle and pulled him closer in a side hug. In response, he lifted his arm and wrapped it around her shoulders so she could lean against him.

"This is the special project you've been constantly sneaking off to work on for the past two weeks."

"Happy birthday." His smile was back.

Jenna let go of him and then ran toward the stairs to the lower platform, with Toby laughing at her heels. If she closed her eyes, she could imagine they were teenagers again, swapping secrets under the stars here. But reality was even better than that image. They were adults, and Toby was home where he belonged. He was attentive and sweet and loved God, and he was good with Kasey and her father, and he was staring at her with the goofiest lopsided grin.

And even though she knew she had to be satisfied with being only his friend for the rest of her life, she'd never wanted anything more than to kiss that man in this moment.

Instead she turned to face the last of the sunlight. Pinks and oranges burst on the horizon, making the trees in the orchard look like they were on fire.

"Come eat," Toby said. He hauled one of the large apple baskets from a stool and began unpacking. There were glass bottles of pop, plates and utensils, food packed in little jars, and a brown box from Gran's Candy Shoppe, a place located in downtown Goose Harbor that served homemade sweets.

Jenna dropped down onto the stool next to him. "You even packed food?"

"These jars have chili with a layer of corn bread baked on top." He tapped the medium-sized jars and then moved on to the larger ones, which obviously held salads. "And these are pear-and-walnut salad. I hope you like that sort of thing. And we have cupcakes for dessert. Red velvet. That's still your favorite, right?"

"Tobe." She'd tried his cooking before and had lived to tell about it, but he still wasn't good with anything more complex than scrambled eggs. "I know you're not much of a cook. Did you make all this?"

"Such doubt." He threw his head back and laughed. "You know me too well. I called up your friend Kendall, and she paired me with one of the caterers she uses for her business. Also, you'll be happy to hear that Kasey and your dad are excitedly waiting for their pizza delivery. I've been informed they have grand plans for a checkers competition, as well as an old-time black-and-white-movie marathon."

Jenna picked up one of the cloth napkins and spread it over her lap. Her shoulder brushed his in the process. "You thought of everything."

His eyes were so warm in the candlelight. "I just wanted you to have a nice evening."

"Well, you picked great company." She elbowed him in the ribs. "But seriously. This is amazing. I can't believe you did all this. It's so much work."

"I did it for you. I'd gladly do more." He passed her a pop and jars of each of the food. "Can I pray for us?"

"Please." She rested a hand on his knee and bowed her head.

"God, we thank You for old roots and new beginnings. I thank You especially for Jenna today, on her birthday. God, she is a blessing to everyone she meets, and without realizing it, she's a beacon of Your hope to the people around her. Bless this food—that I did not cook. Amen."

As they ate, they fell into the usual chitchat about the operation of the orchard, and they brainstormed a list of things they needed to accomplish in the next few days. It was already the beginning of October, and traffic was bound to pick up even more and carry steadily until the end of the month. By November, most of their business would drop off, except for the occasional barn or property rental. This winter they'd host Kendall and Brice's reception, but beyond that, they had nothing else booked yet.

Toby laid down his silverware. "Speaking of this week, I wanted to talk to you about something."

She pushed her plate to the center of the table and turned toward him. "Go on."

"Saturday is our homecoming game. My team at the high school, that is. But it's *our* homecoming game, too." He pointed between the two of them. "They're hosting a party afterward for our ten-year reunion."

Jenna laced her fingers together and studied them. When she received the invitation to the class reunion in the mail, she'd promptly torn it into twenty shreds. Surely Toby knew that she wanted nothing to do with that place and those people who had ridiculed her. He might have fond memories that he wanted to revisit, but she definitely didn't. "I hadn't considered going."

"It would mean a lot to me if you came to the game. My guys have been working hard, and I'd love for you to see the other place I spend my time."

He didn't get it.

"I don't like that place."

"Jenna—I'll be with you." He inched closer. Sometimes it was aggravating how well he could read her, see her fear even when she was trying to mask it. "I have to go, and I don't want to be there without you."

"You want me to go with you?"

"Yes." His goofy grin returned. "I'm apparently botching it, but I'm trying to ask you out on a date."

"Then I'll go." The response was automatic. But even as she said the words, worry found a foothold in her mind. What if she had to face those people? What if Toby's presence didn't make a difference?

"You will?" He sounded so hopeful.

There was no way she could take it back now. "If you want me to."

"I really do." He reached for his pop, and she caught a good look at his hands.

"You have blisters."

"I'm not used to wielding a hammer for that many days straight. Also, I have to come clean and tell you that I didn't do this alone. Evan helped a lot." He looked down at his hands and shrugged. "They'll heal."

Emotion balled in her throat. Toby had spent countless hours building her a tree house to remind her of their childhood together, of all they'd shared and been through. He worked tirelessly for Dad at the orchard and still found energy to give Kasey piggyback rides, help her tackle homework or play a board game with her. Jenna would never—could never—love another man besides this one, and right now, under the glow of candlelight, she had to find out what it felt like to kiss him.

Just once.

Hesitation making her movements slow, she brought her fingertips to trace the stubble along his jawline.

Toby drew in a sharp breath. "Jenna."

"Kiss me." It was less than a whisper.

"Do you mean it?" He sounded hoarse. His eyes searched hers.

"Kiss me, Toby."

He held her gaze as he leaned in, his lips brushing hers. His touch was gentle, but it was everything. Toby started to break away, but Jenna didn't want the moment to end. She looped her arms up around his neck and pulled him toward her again. The feel of sandpaper from stubble lining his jaw lightly scuffed her chin as he tilted his head and kissed her back, stronger and firmer this time. It was warm and sure and right, and everything Jenna had always hoped a kiss with him would be.

When they finally parted, Toby was breathing as hard as Jenna's heart was racing.

His eyes raked over her face, memorizing her, and the muscle on his jaw ticked.

Not sure what to say, Jenna scooted back on her stool. She would cherish this kiss with Toby as the single best moment of her life. A dream come true, if only for a minute.

However, she wasn't delusional enough to believe Toby loved her. He'd been overly kind ever since finding out about Ross. He seemed bent on doing penance for his behavior in high school. They were friends again— true and real friends—and he might have asked her to go with him to their homecoming reunion, but again, she knew how Toby worked. He was righting a wrong. He'd keep her at his side all night as he mingled with the people who had made her life miserable, letting them know they were buddies and always had been. That was all.

He'd kissed her because she'd asked. Turning her down in that moment would have fed the awkwardness in their relationship that they'd been working hard to overcome.

Toby was a nice guy who happened to be an excellent kisser. And he was her friend. End of story.

He leaned closer, regaining the space she'd created, and scooped up her hand. "Jenna, I wasn't planning on saying all this tonight, but I feel like I should now."

Tears gathered in her eyes. He was about to give her the "I really like you as a friend, and that was a mistake" talk. Wasn't he? He'd want to discuss how to reestablish the lines in their friendship, and she didn't want to go through that. Not now, while she was still turning over the memory of their kiss like a precious ruby.

"My time here at the orchard has been the best of my life," Toby said. "Back when I was a kid and also here, now, with Kasey and you. You need to know. Jenna, I—"

She pressed her free hand over his mouth.

Jenna, I want to be your friend. Nothing more.

Jenna, I care about you, but not like that.

Jenna, I can't ever do that again. Understood?

"Please. Please don't say it." Her voice shook. "Don't put us through a long-drawn-out talk. Can't we just leave tonight as a nice little moment without ruining it?"

His brow bunched. "You don't even know what I'm going to say."

"I do, and I don't want to go down that road right now."

He withdrew his hand from hers. "If that's how you feel."

"It is. I'm sorry. I shouldn't have asked you to kiss me. I wasn't thinking. I don't want to hurt our friendship."

He slid away from her and started repacking the basket. Dishes clanked together, and the glass jars pinged as he dropped them in none too carefully.

She stood there watching him, wanting to say something but knowing it wasn't possible when she felt like she was being ripped in two. *Why, God? Why bring him back if it's going to be like this?*

She would surrender her love for Toby to God. Surrender it every day for the rest of her life, because it wasn't going away anytime soon.

Once the basket was packed and ready, he turned to her and added softly, "I'll always be your friend, Jenna. No matter what." He brushed past her and headed down the stairs.

Jenna followed behind him. "I'll always be your friend, too."

And she meant it. No matter how bad it hurt.

Chapter Twelve

The marching band blared the school's favorite fight song, muffling the sound of the announcer counting down the minutes until the break was over. Stadium lights shone over the cheerleaders dancing on the track in front of the crowd. People milled on the bleachers. Some followed along with the cheer squad, imitating the Gator mascot's signature *chomp, chomp, chomp* motion with their arms.

High school smells—roasted hot dogs, popcorn and sweaty football players—should have made Toby feel at home. Still…the adrenaline at a game didn't even come close to how much he enjoyed ending the evening on the back porch swing at Crest Orchard.

Football was an important thread in the fabric of his life story, and he'd always love it. However, it would never define him again. The realization was overdue—long overdue—yet it managed to take him by surprise.

Who was Toby Holcomb?

For much of his existence, that answer had been a revolving door. Football, the boy who lost his brother, popular-crowd ringleader, guy who could get the girl, scholarship winner, business-degree holder, injured, unwanted, failure, drunk, loser.

With all that stripped away…what defined him now?

Pseudo dad to Kasey. Orchard laborer. Man who loved Jenna Crest.

He tightened his grip on the clipboard in his hands, letting the edges bite into his skin.

Once. Just once, he wished a label would stick. *Husband* and *dad* both sounded great these days. Still, those titles depended on other people. His identity needed to be rooted in something that couldn't fall from his hands like football, or deceive him like his old friends, or torment him like the depression, or choose to not be with him, like Jenna.

Saved by God.

Could it really be that easy?

He'd been muddling through his entire life, pretending to be whoever people wanted him to be, when he could have simply been Toby, child of God. That was enough. That was everything. It was a definition that no one could ever take from him, and one that wasn't dependent on him succeeding to maintain it. He could fail and mess up and collapse time and again, and God would still claim Toby as His own.

Toby sighed, feeling as if a weight the size of a high school quarterback had been lifted from his shoulders. Then again, being saved by God also meant that Toby wanted to obey God, which would mean continuing down a path and making choices that honored Him. God was the one who got to shape Toby now, not the opinions of other people.

Final notes from the marching band signaled that the game was about to resume. The Goose Harbor Gators were down by fifteen and had little chance of coming back for a win this late in the game. Still, part of his job was to inspire them.

Toby squeezed the shoulder of one of his players. "Ease up, all right? Don't worry about the score. I was always worried about the score, and look where it got me."

Rob already looked defeated. He pounded back a swig of his electric-blue sports drink and then wiped the dribble off his chin with the back of his hand. "Being like you is hardly a bad thing. It got you almost to the NFL."

"*Almost* doesn't cut it, I'm afraid." A couple other players leaned closer to get in on the conversation. "Besides, my life is better now than it ever could have been if I had achieved my goal and gone pro. Getting injured? That was probably the biggest blessing in my life. Took me a long time to come to that conclusion, but it's true."

"Don't know, Coach. You should probably go see the team trainer and have him take your temperature. You might be getting sick."

Toby cradled his clipboard, confused but used to the constant change of subject when he talked with the high school athletes. "I feel fine."

"But you're talking all cray-zee." Rob made the universal crazy symbol, driving home his point. "Picking apples and lecturing our lazy hides is not better than going pro. No way. I don't believe you for one second."

Caleb Beck, who'd taken over as head coach for the season, glanced over at them but must have heard their conversation and decided they could continue, because he didn't call them over to his huddle. The teenagers Toby spoke with were players who made up the last string of the team. Most of them had seen little game time so far. Caleb's main concern would be those heading onto the field.

"I'm serious." Toby got into a crouch so some of the other players could gather around him. A twinge of discomfort lanced through his knee—he'd ice it later. "Listen, wanting to play sports is a good thing, but keep the option open for other things, too. Life often doesn't go according to plan. Be ready for that. A closed door ended up being the best thing that ever happened to me."

He glanced over the boys' heads to where Jenna sat in the stands with some of her friends. She was radiant tonight, under the lights, wearing her cowboy boots, a dark top, a dangling pair of earrings and her hair swept up in some clip thing. It was a good thing he had to turn his back on the crowd in order to coach because he'd never have been able to focus with her in view. As it was, Toby wanted to call her over to the fence and steal a kiss in front of everyone—wanted to show that she was with him and he was proud of her.

Not gonna happen.

Jenna said their kiss was a mistake. She wished it never occurred. It would have hurt less for her to kick him in his bum knee.

The only mistake on Toby's end was when they'd stopped kissing.

Rob jutted his thumb to indicate where Toby was looking. "You're just saying all this stuff because you've got a hot girlfriend."

Toby let out an exasperated laugh. "I'm saying it because I get to have such *enlightening* conversations with brutes like you." He tapped Rob's knee with his clipboard. "And show a little respect, all right? Don't talk about women like that."

"What? Jenna's hot. We all think so." He looked around for teammate support and got a bunch of nods and grunts in response. "Why is that wrong to say?"

Toby caught Jenna's eye and smiled at her, even though doing so felt akin to dropping his heart into a blender. She didn't want him. Not like he wanted her.

Focus on the players.

"There's a lot more to her—to all women—than their looks. The sooner you learn that, the happier a man you're going to be." Knowing that years ago would have changed his entire course in high school. He would have been with Jenna, and he wouldn't have been stupid enough to ever let her go. His mistakes in college and after, as well as the terrible nightmare she'd lived through her sophomore year, could have been prevented if he'd been man enough to own up to his feelings about her all those years ago.

Because truth was, he'd always been in love with Jenna Crest. He'd just been too scared to allow himself to acknowledge it.

"So you *don't* think she's hot?" another player chimed in. "You're blind, man."

Toby pinched the bridge of his nose and closed his eyes. *Give me words. Give me patience.* "She's the most attractive woman I've ever met, but that has far more to do with who she is and the man she makes me want to be than an image in the mirror."

"Sure, but it doesn't hurt that she's easy on the eyes." Rob wiggled his eyebrows.

"Fine. I give." Toby tossed out his hands. "I'm still a man. She's gorgeous."

"So you two are dating? Because Caleb says you ain't." That tidbit came from Jeffrey, a youth with big dreams, fire-red hair and no body weight.

The buzzer sounded, but Rob and the others still looked at him expectantly. Toby didn't owe the seventeen-year-olds an answer. And he couldn't give the answer he wanted to. He'd love to claim Jenna as his girlfriend. Especially after their kiss...

He shook his head, trying to banish the feel of her lips on his, her sweet lavender smell and the pressure of her arms tugging him closer. Impossible. It was all seared into him.

However, she'd shushed him right when he was about to tell her he loved her. She might as well have shoved him off the top of the tree house and then kicked him a couple times once she climbed down. And lit the clubhouse on fire while she was at it.

Jenna didn't love him. Didn't even want to hear that he loved her.

Was she still skeptical of all males? It would be understandable after what she'd endured with Ross. Even thinking of the man caused Toby's fist to bunch. He'd asked Jenna if she'd ever reported Ross's crimes to the police, and it turned out that she hadn't. At first, she'd been too scared and more concerned with fleeing the situation. She hadn't wanted to face him if that meant going to court to testify. A few years into her healing, she'd considered making a delayed report, but discovering he was married with young twin boys made Jenna abort that plan. She hadn't wanted to destroy his wife's life or take a father away from his children.

Toby didn't know how he felt about the fact that she had never sought justice through the law. Then again, he'd been the one to tell her that ultimately, justice came from God. If Jenna's choice was to never report what happened, Toby would honor that without bugging her. More than anything, Jenna needed that from men—respect. So he'd respect her choice to not file a report, along with respecting her decision to not pursue anything romantic with him. Even though every cell in his body was clamoring for him to fight for her.

Fight and win her.

Jenna helped gather her friend Paige's bags as Paige sent a text message to her sister-in-law, Shelby, who was watching Noah.

The Gators had lost, which wasn't a shocker. The high school team had been nothing to write home about for years.

"I'm sorry." Paige tucked her phone away. "I've morphed into the zany mama people write snarky blog posts about, haven't I? Poor Shelby is probably busier answering me than taking care of my sweet baby."

Jenna batted her hand. "Joel's there, too. He can cover rocking duty while Shelby answers you."

"That's hilarious!" She chuckled. "I'm sure it's exactly what's happening. He really is great with kids. I sure hope he proposes to Shelby one of these days." Paige looped a giant canvas bag over her shoulder. "I think I'll head down and wait outside the locker room. Want to join me?"

"I'm supposed to go to the ten-year reunion shindig with Toby." Jenna peeked over her shoulder, studying the path that trailed around the building to where the party was being held.

"He's probably over there already. Caleb planned

to keep the postgame talk quick—he promised me he would so we could get back home before all the teens go out onto the road." Unfortunately, homecoming and other high school celebrations often meant students drinking and making poor choices. The Goose Harbor police officers were already milling the crowd. "I know for a fact that he planned to let his assistant coaches out right away."

Jenna checked her phone to see if Toby had sent her any texts. Nothing. "I should probably head over there."

Paige gave her a quick hug. "Have fun!" she called as she headed toward the gym.

Jenna wrapped her arms around her middle and picked her way out of the bleachers. Large arrows pointed the way across the grass to a gigantic event tent on the other side of the school, away from the hubbub of the football game. Inside, a crooning band played, and tables covered with crisp white linens lined a wide dance floor. Candles highlighted the framed signs resting at the center of each table denoting the reunion numbers. Five years. Ten years. Fifteen. Twenty. Twenty-five.

She spotted Toby right away. He had his back to her, but she recognized the firm line of his shoulders and the strong way he held himself despite the fact that she knew his knee still bothered him every day. She would know him anywhere. In any crowd. She had him memorized.

Unfortunately, she also knew the people he was talking to. Chad, Nick, Jeremy, Megan and Ashley—his old crew. The people who had tormented her the most. Chad used to walk behind Jenna in the hallways mooing. She still didn't know why. Megan was the one who'd purchased white Amish caps in bulk online and handed them out to all the other girls to wear on the same day to make fun of her.

There was no way she could face them.

Strength is a choice.

Jenna grabbed the back of a folding chair nearby, steeling herself. *Choose strength.* She lifted her chin. *Choose strength.* She started walking across the dance floor to come up behind Toby and join him. *Choose strength.* She was not a victim.

Jeremy cuffed Toby on the back. "Rumor is, you're with her these days. Is that right?"

"Wait, you're with Amish Chick?" Ashley's voice rose in disbelief.

Jenna's feet turned to concrete.

"She's not Amish." Toby jammed his hands into his pockets. "And yeah, I'm living at their place. It's a good job."

"Living at their place"? Not..."She's my best friend"?

"But she was such a zero in high school," Ashley said.

Toby pulled his hands from his pockets to cross his arms over his chest, biceps popping. "She's not—"

"Harsh, Ashley." Megan swirled her drink around in her cup. "We're adults now."

"Anyway." Toby rocked on his feet, clearly uneasy. "No, we're not together. It's not like that. Not at all."

Megan snorted. "Of course not. You and her? Yeah, that's a never."

Jenna dashed away a stray tear. *Stupid.* She was so stupidly stupid to have believed they were friends again. To believe they had *ever* been friends. Toby was ashamed to admit he knew her. She backed away, slamming into a man who looked like he was there for his forty-year reunion.

"Sorry. Sorry." She spun away from him, pinballing between people as she rushed outside.

Get away. Get away before they see you.

Toby didn't care. It had all been a lie. Their friendship wasn't real. Never had been. She was a way to pass his time and nothing more.

One loud sob tore its way out of her throat before she was able to rein in her tears and stumble away from the tent. Strength would have been facing those people—facing Toby—then and there. But Dad was wrong. It wasn't something a person could just choose or summon up upon need. Someone was either strong, or they were not. And Jenna fell firmly into the latter category. Who even cared? Strength mattered very little when it felt like her heart was being shredded apart.

She'd handed him her last piece of hope, and he'd drop-kicked it into the dirt. Again.

The only person she could blame was herself. Toby was a fake. He'd always been a fake. She'd been a fool to believe otherwise.

Claire Atwood held up her hand, waving at Jenna. She called, "Are we still a go for tomorrow?"

Oh, Jenna did not want company right now. She wanted to wallow alone in her heartache.

"Tomorrow?" Jenna eked out.

Claire bid the group of people she was talking to goodbye and then joined Jenna on the bus lane in front of the high school. "Kasey's coming to my place to play with Alex. Don't you remember? I talked to you and Toby at church about it last week. We're going to decorate cookies."

"You'll have to check with Toby." Her voice shook on his name. "I don't have any say with Kasey."

Claire's brow formed a V, and then she hooked her arm through Jenna's and tugged her away from the crowd, down into the parking lot. They stopped between a conversion van and a large bus. "What's wrong? You look like you're going to cry."

Jenna hugged her stomach. "It's nothing."

"It'll help if you tell me." Claire inched closer and lowered her voice. "Is it man troubles?"

"You could say that." She blew out a long stream of air. Perhaps wallowing alone wasn't wise. That route had never helped—it often left her stuck, roadblocked by her own pain. Jenna needed to start reaching out to other women for friendship, especially since she was a terrible judge when it came to men.

"It's Toby, isn't it?" Claire leaned in. "I may be older, but Goose Harbor isn't all that big. Between you and me, I happen to have a good read on these sorts of things. I figured you two had something going on."

"I always liked him but…" She shrugged.

"But he's an idiot." Claire started talking with her hands, causing the mess of bracelets on her wrist to clank. "He hurt you before and now he's done it again, hasn't he?"

"I can't blame him." Jenna moved her arms to cross over her chest and leaned her head against the school bus. If she looked up at the first stars, she might be able to keep her tears from falling. "He doesn't love me. He's never going to." Her own bitter laugh surprised her. "He doesn't even want to be my friend. I'm the idiot."

"You're not." Claire grabbed her biceps with more force than Jenna would have given the lean woman credit for. "If he can't see how amazing you are, that's his huge loss. I'm going to go ahead and give you some advice—woman-to-woman—as a girl who's been down a similar path." She pointed at Jenna with her keys. "Don't let a man with a hold on your past ruin your future. You're better than that. Guys who let women like us go—they just aren't worth our time."

"Toby and I were never involved." Well, other than the one kiss, but that didn't count. She'd all but begged him to kiss her, which wasn't romance. It was pathetic.

Ouch.

Jenna shoved her palm into her sternum, as if the action could hold her crumbling world together.

"Anyway, he's a loser," Claire said. "They *all* are. How about we get out of here and go for ice cream? There's this place I found. It's off the beaten path over in Shadowbend. You're going to love it."

Jenna glanced back at the crowd.

Claire jiggled her arm to gain Jenna's attention. "You know you want to. Come on—my parents are watching Alex, and you're free. I'd love to hang out with you. We've never done that. It'd be nice to get to know you better."

Jenna didn't want to go back to the reunion or find Toby. What would she say to him? He wouldn't miss her. In fact, he'd probably be happy not to have to carry on the charade of liking her in front of all of them.

That thought made her decision easy. Jenna pulled out her phone, sent Dad a message telling him she was bailing on the reunion but was fine and then turned her phone off completely.

"Let's get out of here."

Chapter Thirteen

Hands clutched at the back of his neck, Toby paced the length of the Crests' kitchen. "We need to call the police."

Thankfully, he'd put Kasey to bed more than an hour ago. She'd asked about Jenna no less than ten times before he tucked her in and they said prayers. Fear was front and center in Kasey's eyes—fear that Jenna wouldn't come home, just as her mom hadn't.

Mr. Crest shook his head. "She sent me a message saying she was fine."

"That was hours ago." Toby tugged on his hair. "What if something happened to her? She never showed up to the reunion. I searched the place." Each minute she wasn't there made his pulse rocket. *Where are you, Jenna?* "I walked every aisle in the parking lot looking for her car, and it wasn't there. I've sent her a stalker-level amount of text messages, and my calls keep going to voice mail. This isn't like her."

Her dad scrubbed his hand back and forth over his whiskered chin. "Son, the fact is—"

"If you don't want to call the cops, I get it." Toby

stopped pacing to fish his keys from his pocket. "But I have to go out looking for her, or I'll lose my mind worrying. I… If she's hurt somewhere…if she's alone…"

Mr. Crest laid his hands on the table. It was a silent "Cool your jets." "Being around so many people, she probably had an anxiety attack."

"But why didn't she send me a message?" Toby stared at his phone, willing a message to appear. "I would have left in a heartbeat. I didn't care about that thing. The whole point was to stand there with my arm around her in front of everyone—to help close the door on what tore us apart in high school. I wanted her to get out and have a fun night."

"I'm afraid sometimes when she goes into this zone, she does things that don't make sense," Mr. Crest said. "It's understandable if her behavior bothers you. It's hard to take, and even more difficult to know how to deal with it. There's no shame in admitting that."

"But that's not it at all." Toby held the keys hard enough to leave an imprint on his skin. "I love her—no matter what. She could battle this stuff every day for the rest of her life, and it only makes me see her as strong, a fighter. It's only…" He yanked a chair from the table and dropped down into it. "I want to be there for her. I wish she'd let me. I want to hold her hand through the bad times. Every single one of them."

Mr. Crest fought a smile.

Toby rested his arms on the table. "You heard me right. I love your daughter. I love her so much I can't get through a minute without thinking about her."

"I know that. I've known it for a long time. But it's still nice to hear that *you* finally know it."

Gravel churned outside. Toby shot out of his chair,

knocking it to the floor, and ran to the back door. The sight of Jenna's car parked in its usual spot made him brace his hand against the wall as a shudder of relief worked through his body. Then he plowed out the door and took the back stairs in two leaps, jogging over to her as she exited her car. He pulled her into a hug. "I was so worried."

Her entire body went stiff. "Let go of me."

"Jenna?" He pulled back from her a little. "Where were you?"

She shoved from his hold and stalked out of his reach. "I don't understand you. I never will. Maybe I don't want to. I mean, do you get some sick pleasure out of toying with me?"

Toby felt like he'd been hit upside the head. He was so confused. "What are you talking about?"

"You want to know where I was?" She crossed her arms, the toe of her shoe tapping out her annoyance.

"We can start with that." Then maybe move on to why it looked like she wanted to claw him.

"I went to the reunion." She spoke in a deathly even voice. "Which, for the record, did you only ask me to go to so you could embarrass me more?"

He took a step in her direction and put up his hand, as if he were approaching a growling coyote caught in a trap. "Jenna, I have no idea—"

"Don't." She spit out the word and put up a finger. Her nostrils flared. Her chest rose with a deep breath. "Stop lying to me. That's all you do."

"I've only ever been honest with you." Toby kept his voice as calm as possible, even though he wanted to fight. "You're the only person I can claim that with."

"I *heard* you, Toby." She was yelling now. "They

asked about me, and you denied that we're friends. You denied that we're close. You were ashamed to even say you know me."

At the reunion? But he'd told them that she was amazing. He'd told them they were wrong about her and always had been. He'd even told them he was in love with her and hoped to win her affection someday. Evidently, she'd left before hearing that part.

"That's not what happened at all."

"I am not deaf," she said through clenched teeth. Her eyes were blazing.

"Maybe not, but you're sure bent on only hearing what you want to hear." His voice carried a dangerous edge now, but he couldn't stop it. She'd accused him of lying when she was the one leading him on and tossing him to the side. "Apparently you want to cling to being a victim more than you're willing to see the truth about how I feel about you."

She worked her jaw from side to side. He'd struck a nerve. "You said we're not involved at all."

He groaned. "They were asking about dating, and last I checked, we're not. In fact, last I checked, I'm the joke around here." He thumped his chest. "I'm the one following you around like a puppy hoping you'll notice me, hoping you could care about me, when obviously that's never going to happen. We kiss and—"

"A kiss I had to *beg* for." She got in his face, and even with anger simmering between them, he wanted to kiss her again in that moment.

Instead he took a step back, speaking low. Praying she'd see reason. "A kiss I'd been wanting for a long time, but I waited until you were ready. After everything you've been through, I thought that was the honorable thing to do."

"Oh, I forgot. You're so honorable." She threw out her arms in an encompassing way. "You go around kissing women whenever they ask you to, even though it doesn't mean anything to you. We've got ourselves a real knight in shining armor here, folks."

Her words hurtled through him as if they were jagged rocks, cutting, bleeding, aching. Wounds that would be a long time healing. How had everything gone so wrong? *Fess up. Tell her the truth. Even if it hurts. Even if she laughs in your face.*

Toby closed his eyes and swallowed. "After that kiss, I tried to tell you that I'm in love with you. I want to be with you. The only thing I want—"

"Stop." She held up her hand and stepped backward, using her other hand to grope for the railing that led to the porch. "You're heartless. I can't believe a word that comes out of your mouth." Her voice shook, and the moonlight revealed tears trickling down her chin. "You act one way to me and one way to everyone else. That's the exact opposite of love."

"You're the only person in the world who knows me fully." He reached for her. He couldn't lose her. Not like this. Not over a miscommunication. "Jenna, I love you. Please believe that."

"I don't know you at all." She shrank away from his outstretched hand and fled up the steps. At the top, she looked back down at him. "You're a fake, Toby. That's all you'll ever be."

Then she shoved through the door, and he crumbled onto the steps.

* * *

Jenna skirted around a tipped-over chair in the kitchen and ran past Dad. "I can't talk right now."

"I heard you two."

"Dad—I can't." She kept her head down and made a beeline for the stairs. Toby might follow her in, and she couldn't deal with that. Their back-and-forth just now had zapped all her energy. She was empty now. The only thought in her mind was curling under her blankets for the next two months.

Jenna pounded up the stairs and reached for her doorknob, but a little body came barreling into her, throwing her off balance for a second. Kasey clung to her middle, bawling into Jenna's stomach. Jenna wrapped her arms around the small girl, pulled her into the bedroom and closed the door. She eased Kasey toward her bed and flipped on the small light on her nightstand. The glow cast shadows around them, as if the place where they stood hanging on to each other was the only safe spot in the world.

Jenna dropped to her knees and framed Kasey's face with her hands. "Sweetheart, what's wrong? Why are you awake?"

"You. Hate. T-Toby!" she wailed. "You hate him."

They'd been loud enough for Kasey to hear in her bedroom?

"Oh, Kasey." Jenna pulled her into a bear hug.

"I h-h-heard you." She was crying so hard she could barely get a word out.

"I'm so sorry we woke you."

"Where will I live?" Her lips trembled. "When you toss us out? Where will Toby and I go?"

Sickness rolled through Jenna's stomach. "No one is tossing anyone out."

"But that's what h-happens. People stop loving each other, and they make you leave. Guys always tossed Mom and me out."

"I love you." Jenna stroked her fingers through Kasey's hair, praying she could ease her fears. "Please know that. No one is making you leave."

"But you could stop loving me, just like you stopped loving Toby." Kasey pulled her chin into her chest and hugged herself.

The sight of the small child huddled inward, believing that no one loved her when she was surrounded by love, broke Jenna in two. How could Jenna make Kasey see the truth? She was loved and cherished and wanted. *Be truthful. Even if it hurts.* That was the strength her dad had been referring to all along, wasn't it?

"I haven't stopped loving Toby. I don't think I ever will." Jenna rocked back to sit on her heels. "I'm really hurt and I said some very mean things, but just because he and I aren't together, it doesn't mean I don't care about him. I'm so upset because I *do* love him a lot."

Kasey dragged the sleeve of her nightshirt under her nose. "I wish you two would be married so you could be my mom and dad and I could live with you guys forever."

Not for the first time, Jenna remembered the child she'd lost. The child who would be the same age as Kasey now.

Jenna's chin quivered. "I wish that, too. So much." She swiped at her tears. "I really do. But Toby doesn't know what he wants." That's all she'd say about it. Jenna might be angry with Toby, but she wouldn't paint Kasey's guardian in a bad light. "Sometimes adults get confused about adult relationships. But we both care about you. That's what matters."

Misplaced love was a tornado that destroyed so many people. She shouldn't have let Toby infiltrate her heart again. Look what it was doing to Kasey. This was what Jenna had been afraid of. This was the cost of not keeping her guard up. She hadn't hurt only herself—her behavior had hurt Kasey by getting her hopes up. She could lump her dad into the pile of people she'd hurt, too.

Jenna got off the ground and moved to a chair stationed near her window. She opened her arms, an invitation for Kasey to sit with her. "Come here."

She didn't hesitate. Kasey climbed into her lap, wrapped her arms around her and shoved her warm, tear-streaked cheek into Jenna's neck. "I wish you could be my mom."

Oh, sweet child. I wish that, too.

Jenna cradled Kasey in a tight embrace, rocking slowly as she hummed the same lullaby her mom used to sing to her. Hot tears trailed down her neck, mixing with Kasey's. Jenna cried for the family she'd never have. For the love that ripped into her like a burr. For the child in her arms struggling with feeling lost. And for herself, who felt just as lost and alone as the seven-year-old she was trying to comfort.

Toby had watched the back of Jenna's head all during the church service. She and her dad had taken their own car, leaving without him and Kasey. The new young pastor, Jacob Song, gave an impassioned talk, but Toby was having a hard time concentrating.

After church she avoided him by sequestering herself in a large group of her friends. Toby would have had to burst through their linked arms and interrupt their conversation in order to get to her.

The thought had crossed his mind. More than once.

Claire Atwood held out her hand, eyeing the ladybug backpack he held. "I'm assuming that's Kasey's stuff?"

"Yeah." He looked away from Jenna and focused on the redhead glaring at him. "Thanks for taking her this afternoon. She's been looking forward to it."

"I'll get them both out of kids' club, and we'll head to lunch from here." She slung the loop of the backpack over her shoulder. "My son, Alex, is her biggest fan. He talks more around her than anyone else. We like Kasey a lot."

"Kasey's fortunate to have a friend like him," Toby responded to Claire, but his gaze trailed back to Jenna.

Arms crossed, Claire leaned back to block his view. "Please tell me you're aware that she's in love with you. That once-in-a-lifetime, every-inch-of-her-heart-is-mapped-with-your-image kind of love, right?"

Toby jerked his attention back. Mr. Crest had commiserated with him over the free church coffee a couple minutes ago. During the course of their conversation, he'd told Toby that Jenna had been with Claire when they couldn't find her yesterday. Apparently Claire hadn't been rooting for Team Toby when she was offering advice to Jenna last night. Maybe she'd changed her mind? Whatever the reason, there was no need to play dumb with her.

"If you're talking about Jenna, I think you're probably mistaken. She was very clear about what she thinks of me last night."

"Try this thought on for size for me—you have to love someone greatly to inspire spitting-nails-strength anger. Your emotional pool is only as deep as how you feel about that person to begin with."

He shook his head. Claire hadn't been there. Hadn't heard what Jenna said. "I told her I loved her last night, and she brushed it off."

"If she believes all her dreams have been crushed under the very boots of the man she feels like she can't live without—trust me..." Claire broke eye contact to fiddle with her bracelets. "When you're feeling *that* level of pain, anything's bound to come out of your mouth. From our talk last night, it's clear she thinks you hung the moon. Give her time."

After hugging Kasey goodbye and waving to Pastor Song and his wife as he passed them on the way out, Toby went in search of Mr. Crest and Jenna. Her car was still in the church parking lot, and he wanted to catch them before he left to meet his old friends for lunch. He finally spotted them heading down the ramp on the side of the church.

Gray clouds piled on top of each other in the sky. Deep rumbles echoed across Lake Michigan.

He jogged to catch up and met them as she was unlocking her passenger door. "Here, let me help." He reached to assist Mr. Crest out of his chair and into the seat. They always used the nonmotorized chair for church, since it was smaller and folded into Jenna's trunk easily.

Jenna used her body to block him. "We don't need your help."

He scrubbed his hand over his head. "So we're back to this?"

"If you mean back to being professional, like an employee and employer should be? Then yes. We are." She wedged her hands under her dad's armpits. "Come on, Dad."

"Jenna." Mr. Crest's tone held a warning. She assisted him into the car and closed the passenger door.

Toby grabbed the wheelchair, folded it and hauled it to the back of the car before she could protest. She stomped after him and held open the trunk. Light, chilled rain hit his neck, his face.

He made no motion to put the wheelchair in. "We're not done talking. You don't have to hear me out now, but at some point you'll have to. You can't avoid me forever."

Moisture in the air made her curly hair even curlier, a little wild. Her eyes had a glazed-over appearance to them, as if she was looking past him. Through him. The beacon of light he'd always relied upon had been snuffed out. Was there any hope for them to save their friendship? Her silence made his heart stall.

He cleared his throat. "I won't be back at the orchard until later because I'm meeting Chad and Nick for lunch before they have to head to the airport."

"Well, have fun. You always did enjoy your time with them more than anyone else." She swiped the rain off her forehead.

"Cut me a break here, Jenna. It's not like that."

"Are you going to put Dad's chair in the trunk or should I? It's raining."

He lifted the chair into the trunk. "This is my last chance to talk to those guys. To make any sort of impact and—"

"And it's really none of my concern." She slammed the trunk closed and quickly rounded the car. Within seconds, she was backing it out of its space and leaving him alone in the parking lot, standing in a downpour.

Chapter Fourteen

Jenna leaned over the steering wheel, trying to focus on the road through the downpour. Her wipers screeched on every drag.

When she snapped at Toby in the parking lot, he had looked like he might cry. Tiredness carved lines under his eyes, and his shoulders were sagging. In all the years she'd known him, she'd never seen him standing by like that—completely dejected.

But it was only because his lies had come to light. That had to be it. The other option was too much to hope for—that he really did love her and she was wrong. So terribly, unpardonably wrong about him.

Dad had been quiet for most of the ride home, but he finally sighed loudly. "What did Toby say?"

"He said if you need him, he won't be around until later." Jenna slowed the car to a crawl around the sharp bend where their road wrapped away from Lake Michigan and took them toward the country. Even going ten miles an hour, one of her tires went into the dirt a little. "He's going to go loser it up with his old pals."

Dad folded his hands in his lap. "I've always been

so proud of you and the woman you are, but I can't be right now." He looked out the side window. "Not in this. You're being incredibly unkind."

He didn't get it. All he knew was the Toby from their childhood who smiled and was polite at their dinner table. Jenna hadn't talked much about Toby the Troublemaker. "Dad, those guys were the people who used to get him to go out partying when he was a teenager. They used to sneak out to the beach to drink together. They're the same ones who used to convince him to do so many dumb and bad things. So...sorry, but I'm not exactly going to do a backflip over him crawling back to them."

They bumped up the driveway, and she tossed her car into Park. "Let's wait a bit to see if the rain lets up."

Dad rested his head back on his chair. "Do you know why that man is meeting up with his old friends?"

Jenna glanced at his hands. They were shaky. She needed to set up another appointment for him soon. She yanked her keys from the ignition and dumped them into her purse. "Probably to catch a drink together and talk football."

"Wrong." Dad angled in the chair to better see her. "He knows that neither of them have a relationship with Jesus, and this could be his only chance to ever speak to them about it. Toby set up the lunch last night so that he could tell them about what God has done in his life."

Jenna's mouth felt dry. She licked her lips. "He...he told you that?"

"There is nothing fake about Toby, so you go on and remove that lie from your head." He set his fist down forcefully on the armrest. "That man knows exactly who he is and what God wants him to do with his life. So much so that he's willing to possibly make a fool out of himself to those two old friends today. He was willing to face your wrath over him going to this lunch because he'd rather please God than please you." Dad wagged his finger at her. "Here's my hard, loving truth for you. If there's anyone who isn't being honest with themselves here, it's you, honeybee. Not Toby. That man is as honest as a summer day is long."

Jenna's throat tightened. "Dad?" she squeaked out.

"Hmm?"

"I love him."

"I know that."

A shiver worked its way up Jenna's spine. She wrapped her arms around herself. "I thought he didn't care about me."

"And you need to get to the bottom of why you allowed yourself to believe that. Because that right there is the real issue."

Toby had accused her of something last night. *You want to cling to being a victim more than you're willing to see the truth about how I feel about you.* If what Dad was saying was true—and Dad had zero reason to lie to her, so she knew it was true—then Toby was right. Jenna had chosen to be a victim in her life long before Ross. In high school, when people made fun of her, she had owned their teasing, deciding that they were right. She was weird and lacking and not enough. Someone like Toby could never love her.

When she suffered, God had cared. He'd been with her. He'd wanted to hold her through it and heal her. But Jenna had shoved God away, clinging to the identity of being a victim. If she had allowed God's love to shine into her heart, she couldn't have held on to that any longer. She couldn't have carried the past around as if it were her shield. She would have been required to lay that down and stride forward into the future without the protection of past judgments. She would have had to admit that she was broken and accept however God pieced her back together.

Opening a wound to air always stung, but that was the way it healed, too.

Did Toby really love her, scars and festering wounds and mess that she was? If he did, could she trust it, believing him without second-guessing whether or not she was *worth* loving? Because that's where the real problem was, as Dad had pointed out. The issue wasn't Toby. It was her ability to accept his love.

"Anyone with eyes can tell that boy is crazy about you," Dad said. "He's toiled here all season without complaints, he spends every free minute with you, and when he can't be with you, his eyes follow you or he's talking about you. This house." Dad pressed his hand against the window. The rain had lightened up enough to see outside. "He bartered for all the work to fix it by coaching the football team for free, and he made me agree to let him pay half of the expenses. He wanted to pay the full amount, but I told him I still had some pride left."

"All those hours coaching?" Jenna calculated the hours up in her head. Too many. "He's doing that for free?"

"He's doing them *for you*. And that tree house. Do you know what that man had to do to build that?"

"Daddy, I feel sick over all this." She wiped at her tears. Mascara covered her fingertips. "What have I done?"

"What's done can't be undone, but I have a feeling

that Toby could be persuaded to forgive you. Of course, that'll be after a kiss or two or seven." He winked.

Grateful for Dad's attempt to lighten their heavy moment, she playfully swatted at his shoulder. "You're incorrigible."

"I'm simply an old man who is happy to finally see his daughter deciding to walk in the freedom that comes when you finally open yourself up to love."

"Not yet. I still have to make things right with Toby."

"Wrong again, honeybee. Freedom comes from us choosing to love. Not from someone else's acceptance of it."

Jenna helped her father out of the car, and once they were inside, she got started making them tacos for lunch. While the ground beef simmered, she sent Toby a text: You're right. We need to talk. Looking forward to when you get home.

She debated typing "I love you" but decided that was better kept until she could look him in the eye. After everything, he deserved to hear her say it for the first time.

Hours of checking her phone for a return message, and she'd taken to watching for his SUV out the front window. How long could a lunch be? Surely Chad and Nick's planes would have left by now. The thunderstorm had raged again soon after she and Dad had sat down to lunch, so perhaps their flights had been delayed and Toby was making the most of his extra time.

When her phone rang, she crossed the room in record time and scooped it up. "Hello?"

"May I speak to Jenna Crest?" It was a female voice.

"Speaking."

"Miss Crest, my name is Tonya. I'm a nurse at Saint

Michael's Hospital. A friend of yours has been in an accident—"

"Is it Toby? Toby Holcomb?" Unable to stay standing, Jenna sank into her father's favorite chair.

"He gave us your name as his contact."

Jenna got the information from Tonya but didn't waste time writing anything down. After she'd taken Dad to so many appointments there, every inch of the hospital was familiar to her. Dad was taking a nap in his room, but she shook his shoulder. "Toby's hurt. I don't know how bad. Dad... I haven't told him I love him yet. He doesn't know."

"Keep your head about you. It won't do him any good if you get in an accident on the way there because you're worked up. I'll call Claire and see if they can keep Kasey overnight, so don't you or Toby worry about that. I'll be praying for both of you the whole time."

She pressed a kiss to his temple and headed out, praying in the car the entire drive over. After hastily pulling into a parking spot in the back of the lot, Jenna made a dash through the rain to the automatic doors and gave Toby's name at the front desk. A few minutes later she was shown back to a curtained-off room in the immediate-care section.

"You can go on in. He's been asking for you," the nurse said before heading off.

A police officer spotted her before she could go in with Toby. He filled her in about the accident. "Do you know that blind curve near the lake? It happened there. The other driver was on a motorcycle in the rain. It sounds like he'd gone out for a ride after it stopped the first time and hadn't expected it to start up again so soon. The motorcyclist took the turn too wide. He was traveling in the opposite direction and crossed head-on into Toby's lane on the curve. It's clear that Toby tried to swerve, which was what caused his vehicle to roll. There was nothing he could have done to prevent this. Between you and me, his truck came to rest less than a foot from going over the cliff there."

Jenna steadied herself by placing a hand on the wall. "The motorcyclist?"

The officer looked away. "He didn't make it."

Someone had died tonight. Toby could have easily died. She still didn't know the extent of his injuries. "Was it someone I would know?"

He sighed. "The new pastor. Jacob Song."

Jenna covered her mouth with her hand. "Oh, his poor wife."

"I haven't let Toby know yet."

"I'll tell him. Thank you for all you've done."

Jenna knocked on the edge of the wall before pulling back the curtain. The metal links hooked along the ceiling made a jangling sound as she entered.

Toby was tucked beneath the white sheets of a rolling hospital bed. They'd stripped him of his shirt and put him in one of those huge, ill-fitting gowns that dipped on his shoulder. An IV beeped at the side of the bed. A deep blue color framed his left eye—it would be a full shiner tomorrow—and the patched-up gash near his temple might leave a scar. More bruises dotted what she could see of his shoulder, where his seat belt would have been, and his left arm was covered in wrapping.

He glanced away from the movie he was watching, and a soft, sleepy smile crept onto his face. "You came."

"Of course I came." She crossed to the bed, dropped her purse into the chair and eased to sit on the edge of the bed. He automatically placed his hand on her thigh, and she lightly took his face in her hands and pressed her lips to his. It wasn't the first thing she had originally planned to do, but her emotions took over. Tonight another woman had lost the man she loved. At that thought, Jenna deepened their kiss.

"I love you," she whispered from an inch away. "I've been in love with you since we were thirteen years old swapping secrets in our old tree house." Another kiss.

"Jenna." He breathed her name against her lips.

She pulled away. "I probably shouldn't have started by walking in here and immediately laying one on you."

"It wasn't just one." He smiled. "And I see no problem with what you did."

"How are you?" She ran her fingers down his chest, looking for injuries.

"I was pinned in my truck on its side. There was glass everywhere. It wrapped around a tree on the cliffs there."

Those trees were the only things that had prevented his SUV from going over the cliff and plummeting down onto the beach. Toby would have never known she loved him. All because she'd chosen to believe lies instead of stopping and seeing the truth. Never again.

She would find the right time to tell him that their pastor, Jacob Song, died in the accident, but not right now. She needed to know how badly hurt he was first, and she needed his forgiveness. Then they'd grieve for their pastor together.

He lifted up his gauze-covered arm. "This one's cut up pretty bad, and I have some bleeding on my side and the leg on that side, too. I'm waiting for them to take me to some scan or other to make sure my internals are good. They said a few of my ribs are busted. That's what hurts the most."

Jenna leaned over him, careful not to put weight on his body, and pressed a kiss to his injured arm.

"I could get used to this." Toby laughed—then moaned and braced his hand along his side. "Okay, no laughing. That really hurts."

"Toby?"

He traced his noninjured hand down her arm, sparking a convention of goose bumps on her skin. He took her hand and laced their fingers together.

"I was so cruel to you last night and this morning. The things I said." She shook her head. "I can't take them back, and I wish I could. I was so wrong about you. You're the wonderful one, and I'm working through so much junk. I exploded on you and didn't let you explain yourself. There's no excuse for how I acted." She traced her finger over his knuckles. "Please forgive me."

"Of course I forgive you." He let go of her hand and brought it up to cup her jaw, turning her face to meet his gaze. "But please cut out that 'you're wonderful and I'm not' garbage, because I think you're wonderful, and I've got so much growing to do. But it turns out, that's basically life. We're all dealing with our own messes, and anyone who thinks otherwise is wrong. Love is about coming alongside someone and saying 'I love you, not despite or for your mess, but I love you in the midst of this mess and want to be in it with you.'"

"Sounds like you've been talking to my dad." She straightened his bedsheet.

Toby caught her hand again. "He's a smart man."

"That he is."

"I think I've been in love with you my whole life. I've been trying to tell you for weeks."

Jenna soaked in his words. "You should have grabbed me and kissed me. Swept me off my feet. Anything! If I had known you loved me, nothing would have stopped me from lunging into your arms. I kid you not." Even as she said it, though, she knew it probably wasn't true. Everything had happened at the right time. God had used Dad, Kasey and Toby to chip away at the cave she'd hidden in, freeing her for love. If Toby had professed his feelings for her two or three weeks ago, she might not have accepted it like she could now.

"With everything you've been through, I didn't want to scare you." His words were so quiet, but they struck Jenna hard. Toby had been showing her love the whole time through respecting her and by treating her honorably. To wait for her—to care that much—he was, by and large, the best man she'd ever known.

She pressed her lips to the back of his hand. "The only thing that scares me is picturing a life without you beside me."

"Not a problem. I want to be with you forever."

"I thought you said you weren't interested in dating," she teased.

"I'm not." He bit back a groan as he scooted forward, sitting up farther. He took her chin again and leaned so they were a breath apart. "I'm saying skip that part. Marry me."

She traced her fingers up his jawline, tucking them into the hair at the back of his neck. "I'll marry you right here, right now. Just say the word, and I'll go fetch the on-duty chaplain. Or we could wait until you're strong enough to carry me in the orchard again."

Toby's eyes widened. "So you *were* awake that day."

"Tobe, don't you see? I've been awake since that first day you spooked me by the fence. You do that to me. That's one of the reasons I love you so much." Jenna closed her eyes and met his lips.

"Yeah?" His words heated her cheeks. "What are the other reasons?"

She pressed back, giving him space. He was smiling, but broken ribs had to be painful.

"I'll tell you one a day for the rest of our lives," she promised.

"Here's to a long life, then."

Epilogue

Jenna wrapped her fingers over the doorjamb on the front sliding door to the barn at Crest Orchard and watched the wedding guests inside. It was still light out, as they'd chosen to have an early ceremony, and the reception would end soon. The guests would be gone before sunset.

Lively music pulsed throughout the building. The country band they'd hired was still in full swing, and people were inside mingling, smiling, laughing—having a good time. Even now, standing in the all-white dress that went along with the new diamond band on her finger and her new name, she was having a hard time believing that they'd pulled off planning everything in only three weeks. But the wedding had happened just as she'd dreamed it would all those years ago. She'd married her best friend, Toby Holcomb, under an archway of apple trees.

"Mrs. Jenna Holcomb." She spoke the cherished words for her ears only.

Dad wheeled over to fill the doorway next to her. "You're beautiful, honeybee. More than ever. You downright glowed today. That's the only way to describe it. That boy does that to you. He always has, but today was a wonder."

She rested her hand on his arm as emotion balled in her throat. Dad had saved up his strength all week in order to walk her down the aisle. He'd rotated between crying and grinning all day. Sometimes both at once.

He reached up to set his hand on top of hers.

"I wish Mom were here," Jenna said.

Dad closed his eyes and breathed deeply. "Today would have been her proudest moment. I know it's mine. Not because you weren't fine on your own, but because we both knew early on that God had plans for you and Toby. We used to pray together for both of you. We prayed about this day many times."

It was hard to take in. When she and Toby were still children, her parents had been praying for their future. For years she'd believed that God had turned His back on her life, only to discover He'd been present in every moment. He'd been working through her parents for so many years. Tonight she and Toby would start praying for Kasey together—for her future and for the people that they might not even know yet who would someday impact her life. It was an awesome responsibility—and it was hers. She'd become a wife and mother all in one day.

Jenna scooted to get in front of her dad's chair and leaned in to hug him. "Thank you for showing me such steadfast love and believing God was working in my life. Especially on the days I was at my worst. I wouldn't be here today, whole and able to love Toby like I do, without everything you've done over the years."

"Love is a gift. When viewed that way, it's never hard to give to anyone. Remember that." He peered over her shoulder. "Looks like your friend Maggie is heading this way to collect me. I better find Kasey, too."

Her father and Kasey would spend the weekend at Maggie's inn, which was situated closer to the downtown section of Goose Harbor, leaving Toby and Jenna the orchard for the evening. Tomorrow the newlyweds would head to the airport, and Jenna would board an airplane for the first time in her life to head to their honeymoon.

When Dad returned with Kasey, Jenna kissed her father goodbye and bear-hugged Kasey. "We'll be back before you know it."

Kasey squeezed her with rib-crushing strength. "I'll miss you guys, but Grandpa C says you two have to have time alone, and he's cool and I'll be with him, so that won't be bad."

"Hey." Jenna squatted down to be on eye level with her. "I love you. I love you so much."

"We're a family now, aren't we?" Kasey played with the pale blue ribbon on her dress. "You and Toby will be like my parents now."

Jenna cupped the child's face. "Forever and ever. You're stuck with us."

"I like that." Kasey offered a sheepish smile.

Jenna smoothed her fingers down Kasey's hair. "I *love* it."

"Come on now, Kasey," her dad hollered and motioned for her to join him. "Time to bid our goodbyes to everyone."

As Jenna got to her feet, an arm wound around her stomach and Toby pulled her so her back was snug against his chest when she stood. His jaw brushed through her hair until his lips found her ear and he whispered, "Run away with me."

She melted against him, letting his arms hold her up. "I wish we could."

"Why can't we?"

"There're still people here." She gestured toward the guests in the barn.

"They have cake. They'll be fine without us." Toby turned her in his arms, cradled the back of her neck and pressed a kiss to her forehead. Then he walked his fingers down her arm, scooped up her hand and gave a playful tug as he jerked his head in the direction of the orchard. "Let's get out of here."

"But they all—"

"I repeat—they have cake," he deadpanned while he played with the fingers of the hand he held.

Jenna swatted his chest. "Have I ever told you that you're a rat?"

He caught her other hand. "A time or two. And if I forget, I'm sure you'll remind me." He pulled her against his chest and wrapped his arms around her so she was pinned in place.

She didn't mind one bit.

But the rule follower in her urged her to go play hostess inside the barn. "Shouldn't we?"

"I want to be with *you*." He took a few steps back, bringing them closer to the tree line. "Not them."

Jenna playfully pushed on his chest, feeling the rich fabric of the suit he wore. "You win. Lead the way, handsome."

And just like that, as if they were teenagers sneaking off like the old days, they laughed and started running hand in hand into the orchard.

"I can't keep up." Jenna dropped his hand once they were hidden beyond a few rows of trees. "These shoes." She glared down at her sparkly shoes. They were pretty, but they pinched.

Toby shook his head, a huge smile on his face. "You're so cute when you're frustrated."

"It might not be as cute if that frustration is aimed at you, dear husband of mine."

"Wow. That sounds good. *Husband.*" He closed the distance between them and gave her the kiss she'd been wanting all day. Not the polite kiss couples gave at the altar. No, this one was deep and long enough to get lost in. Jenna wasn't sure she ever wanted to find her way out of their embrace.

When they finally broke apart, Toby pressed his forehead to hers and kept his eyes closed. "I am my beloved's, and my beloved is finally mine. Thank You, God. Thank You for letting us find this day. Thank You for my wife."

In a fluid motion, he bent and lifted her into his arms.

"Tobe! You goof." She circled her arms around his neck and smiled at him. "What are you doing?"

"I'm keeping a promise. You said you wanted me to carry you through the orchard on our wedding day."

"What about your ribs?" They'd married as quickly as they could after his car accident. All his bruises were gone, and for the most part his scrapes and cuts were healed, but the doctor had said it would take a while for his ribs to fully mend. However, Toby had insisted he was well enough and didn't want to wait another week.

"They're fine." Seemingly in no rush to move, he stood between two rows of trees holding her. Despite the autumn chill in the air and the fact that she wore only her dress without a coat, the last afternoon rays of sunlight plus Toby's proximity were enough to keep her warm.

"What do you say, should I carry you home?" Toby asked in a low, rumbly voice.

Jenna gave him a serious look. "I'm afraid you'll have to carry me forever, then."

"I'll carry you anywhere. I'll go anywhere you go. My life is where you are, Jenna. Always."

"Toby, don't you see? Right here. Your arms." She slipped a hand under his suit coat and felt around until she found his heartbeat. This is home." Jenna tilted in his arms to give him a sweet, lingering kiss. "You have made all my dreams come true."

"Ah, but see, that's where you're wrong." Toby winked at her and turned so he could carry her in the direction of their tree house. "I'd say our dream has only just begun."

* * * * *

Pick up these other GOOSE HARBOR *stories
from Jessica Keller:
Love is in big supply on the shores
of Lake Michigan*

*THE WIDOWER'S SECOND CHANCE
THE FIREMAN'S SECRET
THE SINGLE DAD NEXT DOOR
SMALL-TOWN GIRL*

Available now from Love Inspired!

Find more great reads at www.LoveInspired.com

Dear Reader,

Lies are the worst, aren't they? Especially ones we tuck away in our hearts—ones we allow to begin to define us.

Sometimes we're aware of the falsehoods we believe. We repeat them over and over to ourselves when we're hurting. Because of what had happened in his life, Toby believed he was a failure. It stopped him from being able to grow in his relationship with God, and it kept him from understanding his value in the world.

Other times a lie can be buried so deep we don't realize it's there or how much it affects the way we view the world and ourselves. Jenna didn't realize that she believed she wasn't worthy of love, but everything about how she interacted with others showed this to be true. She believed this so much that it blinded her from seeing God was there beside her, fighting for her, loving her.

I'm so glad Toby and Jenna chose to be strong. They're on their way to eradicating the lies that were so comfortable to cling to for so long. That's hard work, friends. I pray you're in the process of doing this, as well. The truth is that God's love for you is not dependent on anything you can do to lose or gain His attention. He loves you. You can choose to believe that or not. That's really all there is to it.

Thanks for walking through a part of Toby and Jenna's love story with me. Make sure to read all the other books in the Goose Harbor series. I love connecting with readers! Look for me on my author Facebook page or on Twitter, or connect with me through my website and newsletter at www.JessicaKellerBooks.com.

Dream big,
Jess Keller

REQUEST YOUR FREE BOOKS!

2 FREE INSPIRATIONAL NOVELS
PLUS 2
FREE
MYSTERY GIFTS

Love Inspired®

YES! Please send me 2 FREE Love Inspired® novels and my 2 FREE mystery gifts (gifts are worth about $10). After receiving them, if I don't wish to receive any more books, I can return the shipping statement marked "cancel." If I don't cancel, I will receive 6 brand-new novels every month and be billed just $4.99 per book in the U.S. or $5.49 per book in Canada. That's a saving of at least 17% off the cover price. It's quite a bargain! Shipping and handling is just 50¢ per book in the U.S. and 75¢ per book in Canada.* I understand that accepting the 2 free books and gifts places me under no obligation to buy anything. I can always return a shipment and cancel at any time. Even if I never buy another book, the two free books and gifts are mine to keep forever.

105/305 IDN GH5P

Name _____ (PLEASE PRINT) _____

Address _____ Apt. #

City _____ State/Prov. _____ Zip/Postal Code

Signature (if under 18, a parent or guardian must sign)

Mail to the **Reader Service:**
IN U.S.A.: P.O. Box 1867, Buffalo, NY 14240-1867
IN CANADA: P.O. Box 609, Fort Erie, Ontario L2A 5X3

**Are you a subscriber to Love Inspired® books
and want to receive the larger-print edition?
Call 1-800-873-8635 or visit www.ReaderService.com.**

* Terms and prices subject to change without notice. Prices do not include applicable taxes. Sales tax applicable in N.Y. Canadian residents will be charged applicable taxes. Offer not valid in Quebec. This offer is limited to one order per household. Not valid for current subscribers to Love Inspired books. All orders subject to credit approval. Credit or debit balances in a customer's account(s) may be offset by any other outstanding balance owed by or to the customer. Please allow 4 to 6 weeks for delivery. Offer available while quantities last.

Your Privacy—The Reader Service is committed to protecting your privacy. Our Privacy Policy is available online at www.ReaderService.com or upon request from the Reader Service.

We make a portion of our mailing list available to reputable third parties that offer products we believe may interest you. If you prefer that we not exchange your name with third parties, or if you wish to clarify or modify your communication preferences, please visit us at www.ReaderService.com/consumerschoice or write to us at Reader Service Preference Service, P.O. Box 9062, Buffalo, NY 14240-9062. Include your complete name and address.

LI15

*Discovering he has a two-year-old son is a huge
surprise for veterinarian Wyatt Harrow. But so are his
lingering feelings for the boy's pretty mom…*

Read on for a sneak preview
of the fifth book in the
LONE STAR COWBOY LEAGUE: BOYS RANCH
miniseries, *THE DOCTOR'S TEXAS BABY*
by *Deb Kastner*.

Wyatt glanced at Carolina, but she wouldn't meet his
eyes.

Was she feeling guilty over all Matty's firsts that she'd
denied Wyatt? First breath, first word, the first step Matty
took?

He couldn't say he felt sorry for her. She should be
feeling guilty. She'd made the decision to walk away.
She'd created these consequences for herself, and for
Wyatt, and most of all, for Matty.

But today wasn't a day for anger. Today was about
spending time with his son.

"What do you say, little man?" he asked, scooping
Matty into his arms and leading Carolina to his truck.
"Do you want to play ball?"

Not knowing what Matty would like, he'd pretty
much loaded up every kind of sports ball imaginable—a
football, a baseball, a soccer ball and a basketball.

Carolina flashed him half a smile and shrugged
apologetically. "I'm afraid I don't know much about

these games beyond being able to identify which ball goes with which sport."

"That's what Matty's got a dad for."

He didn't really think about what he was saying until the words had already left his lips.

Their gazes met and locked. She was silently challenging him, but he didn't know about what. Still, he kept his gaze firmly on hers. His words might not have been premeditated, but that didn't make them any less true. He was sorry if he'd hurt her feelings, though. He wanted to keep things friendly between them.

"There's plenty of room on the green for three. What do you say? Do you want to play soccer with us?"

Shock registered in her face, but it was no more than what he was feeling. This was all so new. Untested waters.

Somehow, they had to work things out, but kicking a ball around together at the park?

Why, that almost felt as if they were a family.

And although in a sense that was technically true, Wyatt didn't even want to go down that road.

He had every intention of being the best father he could to Matty. And in so doing, he would establish some sort of a working relationship with Carolina, some way they could both be comfortable without it getting awkward. He just couldn't bring himself to think about that right now.

Or maybe he just didn't want to.

Don't miss
THE DOCTOR'S TEXAS BABY
by Deb Kastner, available February 2017
wherever Love Inspired® books and ebooks are sold.

www.LoveInspired.com

SPECIAL EXCERPT FROM

Love Inspired HISTORICAL

Forced to marry her father's new employee after being caught overnight in a storm, can Caroline find love with her unlikely husband?

Read on for an excerpt from
WED BY NECESSITY,
the next heartwarming book in the
SMOKY MOUNTAIN MATCHES *series.*

Gatlinburg, Tennessee
July 1887

As a holiday, Independence Day left a lot to be desired. Independence was a dream Caroline Turner wasn't likely to ever attain.

The fireworks' blue-green light flickered over the sea of faces, followed by red, white and gold. She schooled her features and made her way along the edge of the field to where the musicians were playing patriotic tunes.

"Caroline, we're running low on lemonade."

"Then make more," she snapped at eighteen-year-old Wanda Smith.

"We've misplaced the lemon crates."

At the distress in the younger girl's countenance, Caroline relented. "Fine. I'll look for them. You may return to your station."

It took her a quarter of an hour to locate the missing lemons. By then, the last of the fireworks had been shot off and attendees were ready for more food and drink.

The celebration was far from over, yet she wished she could return home to her bedroom and solitude.

A trio of young women approached and engaged her in conversation. As usual, they wanted to know about her outfit, whether she'd had it made by a local seamstress or her mother had had it shipped from New York. Before they'd exhausted their talk of fashion, a stranger inserted himself into their group.

"Excuse me."

Caroline didn't recognize the hulking figure. Well over six feet tall, he was as broad and solid as an oak tree and looked as if he hadn't seen civilization in months. He was dressed in common clothing, and his shirt and pants were clean but wrinkled. Dirt caked the heels of his sturdy brown boots. His thick reddish-brown hair was tied back with a strip of leather. While he appeared to have a strong facial structure, his mustache and beard obscured the lower half of his face. His mouth was wide and generous. Sparkling blue eyes assessed her.

"Would you care to dance?" He spoke in a rolling brogue that identified him as a foreigner.

Don't miss
WED BY NECESSITY by Karen Kirst,
available wherever Love Inspired® Historical books
and ebooks are sold.

www.LoveInspired.com

LIHEXP0117

Love the Love Inspired book you just read?

Your opinion matters.

Review this book on your favorite
book site, review site, blog or your own
social media properties and share your
opinion with other readers!

Be sure to connect with us at:
Harlequin.com/Newsletters
Twitter.com/LoveInspiredBks
Facebook.com/LoveInspiredBooks